9.50

D1336633

DRAW DOWN THE DARK MOON

Four hundred years ago a gipsy cursed the
men of Darrenscar. 'You will come back, in
every century, Blane, and when you and your
brother are together then I will be there . . .
Neither you nor your brother will have any
other light of love, they will die and you will
suffer . . .' And it happened as she said. In
1979, the year of the big freeze, Dee goes to
the lonely house on the Yorkshire moors—
and feels she has been there before. She meets
Charles, her employer, his little boy Richard,
faded Aunt Kitty and her son Alan. When
they are snowed up, Dee knows someone is
practising witchcraft—someone is planning
to kill her.

DRAW DOWN THE DARK MOON

Joyce Bell

'The waning, or dark moon, was the symbol of Hecate, goddess of magic and inspiration. Jason was told by his mother, Aphrodite, to invoke Hecate "to draw down the dark moon" since she herself could not work magic.'

Witchcraft, the Sixth Sense and Us,
Justine Glass.

A Lythway Book

CHIVERS PRESS
BATH

First published in Great Britain 1982
by
Robert Hale Limited
This Large Print edition published by
Chivers Press
by arrangement with
the author
1988

ISBN 0 7451 0729 X

British Library Cataloguing in Publication Data

Bell, Joyce
Draw down the dark moon.
I. Title
823'.9'4 [F]   PR6052.E44/

ISBN 0–7451–0729–X

DRAW DOWN THE DARK MOON

CHAPTER ONE

I knew, even before we reached the brow of the hill, what I was going to see. A large stone-built house, lonely on the Yorkshire moors, with windows like dark closed eyes. Not a happy house, but one where I would live, and where I would be trapped . . .

There had been no sign of the house from the main road, nor from the single track which led to the village. The moors rolled away into the distance, purple, blue and black, with grass golden brown where the October sun touched it, and vivid orange bracken. As we tipped the hill a roof came into view, almost hidden by tall trees, the only trees on the horizon. Then the taxi stopped and the driver said: 'That's Darrenscar.'

He made no effort to come any farther, so I paid him, took my case, and walked the dried mud track to the gate in the stone wall. Inside the enclosure there was no sign that anyone lived there, no name, no trace of the inhabitants, not even a dog. I opened the gate and it was just as I had known it would be, a large imposing building with stone pillars surrounding the front entrance, though the deserted look, the air almost of desolation was new to me.

But why did I feel I knew it so well?

A tremor of unease shot through me. I was not usually so fanciful. Level-headed, Miss Jones had called me in my last year at school. 'Delia is always so level-headed, and quite clever. What a pity she has decided to leave at sixteen.' But it wasn't altogether my decision; I had no fond parents to urge me on to higher things, just an aunt who hoped I'd work as soon as possible. Now, three years later, I was taking a job as secretary cum home help at Darrenscar.

I had not been for an interview. I read the advertisement in the London paper after I'd lost my job. *Girl required for typing author's manuscript and to help with handicapped child. Write to Mr Charles Blane, Darrenscar, Yorkshire.* And, restless after another stormy argument with Aunt Meg, I'd written, determined to break away.

The reply had come within a week. My particulars sounded satisfactory. Would I come immediately, prepared to start, my expenses would be paid. No interview. No reference required. *'You seem to be the girl we are looking for,'* the letter said.

I walked to the great iron-studded door and rang the heavy bell. No need to stay if I didn't like it. I had broken away from my aunt now, I could return to London, live on my own . . .

The door creaked open and a small rosy-cheeked woman stood before me. She looked so kind and homely that I wanted to laugh at my fears.

'Hallo,' I said. 'I'm Delia Martin. Is Mr Charles Blane around?'

'Please come in.' She moved aside, beaming. 'He's in the study. I'll fetch him.'

'Are you the housekeeper?' I asked, curiously.

'Aye, and cook-general as well. Mrs Appleby's the name.' She closed the door carefully behind me, and it was obvious that the front entrance was seldom used. ''Tisn't easy to get girls to work here, you see.'

'Too lonely, I expect,' I said.

'We—ell, the village is only two miles down the road. But girls don't want this sort of work these days, and then—they don't like to come here much.'

'Why not?'

'Because—' it was obvious that Mrs Appleby was as open as the day—'Some funny things went on here at one time and people have long memories in villages. But I'll tell Master Charles.'

She moved into the study and as I watched her I asked myself how I knew it was the study. The house seemed as familiar to me inside as out. I knew the long hall led into the kitchen, that these closed doors hid the drawing-room, the dining-room, the ballroom. There was a fine carved staircase leading to the bedrooms, and

3

along the landing there was a further back staircase up to the servants' attics, and down to the yard outside. *How did I know?*

I've been reading too many murder mysteries, I told myself, seeing too many horror films. That's all it is. Now the master will walk out, tall and handsome, and I'll fall hopelessly in love with him.

He walked towards me, and though tall he wasn't handsome. Nor did I fall in love with him. *But I felt I'd met him before.*

Suddenly it was all too much for me. I felt lost, even a little scared. He shook hands, said a few words of welcome which I answered, but it was through a blur. He must have noticed for he said: 'Mrs Appleby will take you to your room. When you've rested come down at your leisure. We'll have tea.'

And then I was walking up the carved staircase, to the end room on the right, a small room clean and neat, with its single bed with a patchwork quilt, its window looking over the moors, a little writing desk in the corner. So old-fashioned I almost expected to see a wash-stand with jug and basin along the side.

I sat on the bed and Mrs Appleby looked at me in concern. 'You're tired,' she pronounced. 'You'll feel better when you've had something to eat, I expect you've had nothing all day.'

'Mrs Appleby,' I said. 'Has this place ever been used as a boarding house, you know, taking visitors?'

'Why, no.' She stopped, surprised. 'Whatever made you think of such a thing?'

'I just wondered if I'd been here with my parents,' I said. 'When I was small. I seem to remember it.'

She shook her head. 'Never. And I've been working here, on and off, for twenty years.'

'Maybe we came on a visit,' I urged. There had to be an explanation.

'I don't think so,' she said, doubtfully. 'The Blanes haven't gone in much for visitors, not since the war anyway. Oh, there was a time when they used to entertain, and throw their money around, but not for many years. Keep themselves to themselves now, the Blanes.'

I stared out at the lonely moors, the great sky.

'Why don't you ask your mother?' Mrs Appleby said.

'My parents died in an accident when I was six,' I told her.

'Your poor child.' Mrs Appleby was concerned. 'So you're all alone in the world. No sisters or brothers?'

'No. Just Aunt Meg. We didn't get on very well. I always had the feeling that she just took me in out of a sense of duty, being my only relative.'

'Where did you work before you came here?'

'Oh, I had several jobs.' And that had been

another bone of contention between us. 'Why can't you settle down?' Aunt Meg had asked. Why couldn't I? Was there something wrong with me? 'I thought once I'd like to be a nurse,' I said.

'Well now, that would be nice. You could have applied for training now you're what? Nineteen?'

'I did start evening classes,' I said. 'First aid and all that.' And no doubt this had been a decisive factor in my getting this job.

'And yet you come here?' Mrs Appleby's voice was faintly puzzled, and I realised I wasn't giving a very good account of myself. Yet how could I explain my own mixed feelings? How explain to someone, even one so nice as Mrs Appleby, the mixture of liking and rebellion I felt towards Aunt Meg? Times when I remembered that but for her I would have been pushed into an orphanage, when I felt that she was right, I did owe her something, if only a little love . . . Then the rebellion would break out and I'd leave yet another job . . .

'I felt I had to come,' I said. 'When I saw the name Darrenscar, it was as though I'd been waiting for this.'

'Didn't you have a boy-friend?' Mrs Appleby changed the subject. 'You're a pretty girl.'

'No.' I took a fleeting look at my reflection in the mirror on the old-fashioned dressing-table. Reddish brown hair, grey eyes, clear skin.

There had been fellows, several of them, and me, wanting, hoping to fall in love. This is the one, I'd thought as I met Pete or Mike or Gary. This time it's real. But after a few dates Pete or Mike or Gary would turn out to be just another ordinary guy and I'd refuse to see him again, asking myself mockingly what I waited for, the dark romantic stranger, the dream man? And there'd be another row with Aunt Meg, and another job. 'You're just as hard as nails,' she would say as I flounced out. She never realised that I was unhappy, longing for something, hardly knowing what it was I wanted.

I walked to the window. Beyond the yard and outbuildings a long grassy field stretched to the edge of the moor.

'This isn't a farm, is it?' I asked. 'I noticed a lot of sheep on the moors.'

'Oh, no. There was a farm belonging to the estate and the Bradshaws always worked it. Then the Blanes sold it to 'em some years back when they needed the money. But Jim Bradshaw still sees to our sheep, him and young Alan. There's no livestock at Darrenscar except the chickens Mrs Blane keeps.'

'I see.'

'But I'll go down now and make the tea. The bathroom's at the end of the passage.'

'Is it?' I hadn't known where the bathroom was.

'Aye. Mr Blane had some modernising done a

few years back. But I must go.'

She left, and I unpacked my case, washed and changed. Then I went thoughtfully to the stairs.

It was a beautiful staircase, hand-carved, and at the top and bottom were four large carved animals. I looked at them, made to touch, drew away. I had the feeling that one of them was loose, could be lifted right off . . . but I dare not touch them to find out if it were true.

Slowly I walked down to meet the master.

*   *   *

He was waiting in the hall and led me into the kitchen, a large low room with exposed beams and a gap along one side where an old range had been. Along another wall stood an oak dresser holding blue-rimmed plates, while opposite, a new window had been inserted, giving marvellous views of the moors. The back of Darrenscar was much more pleasant than the front, I decided. No doubt the front rooms were closed, unused.

'We eat here,' Mr Blane confirmed my thought. 'It's easier for all of us. Mrs Appleby doesn't live in, and there's no bus, so she's dependent on a lift to get her home. Do sit down—er—Miss Martin. Or do you prefer Delia?'

'Neither,' I said. 'I'm always known as Dee.'

'Well then, Dee, would you like to pour?'

The cups were china, yellow daffodils on a white background. I handed one to my employer, taking a good look at him as I did so. He'd be about thirty, I judged, though his face was harsh and lined, his hair dark and springy, and there was an expression on his face I could hardly fathom. Bitterness? Cynicism? He saw my glance and asked. 'Are you feeling better now? I hope you are strong.'

'Very strong,' I replied. 'Please tell me what I'll have to do.'

'First of all there's the typing. My books are mostly historical. At the moment I'm doing a history of Darrenscar.'

'I'd enjoy that,' I said, really meaning it.

'The house is very old, seventeenth century. And my family have been here from the start.'

'So it's really a history of your family?'

'Yes.' He saw my interest and went on. 'The first Charles Blane made himself a fortune in London, then brought his ill-gotten gains up here.'

'Ill-gotten?'

'The man was a robber.'

I looked perplexed, and there was a mocking amusement in his grey eyes. 'Oh, no, he wasn't a pick-pocket; he did things on a grand scale, much the best way if you want to make a fortune. When London grew too hot to hold him he came here, did a favour for a local

9

big-wig who sold him this land, and built Darrenscar.'

'You don't sound very fond of your ancestors,' I remarked.

'Should I be? Are you fond of yours?'

I thought of Aunt Meg, and was silent.

'The Blanes were a rough, roistering lot,' he said. 'Given to violence.'

'And you want to write about them?'

'Yes, but not because I love them. And it won't be a genteel, school-missy account of charming make-believe heroes, I warn you.'

'Why are you writing it then?'

'Ah.' He looked at me as though assessing me in some way. 'I'll perhaps tell you later.'

The words were dismissive, as though he wanted to change the subject, but I couldn't leave it. I said. 'But you're not a violent man, how could you be, if you are a writer?'

'You don't know,' he said, and a spasm of something like pain crossed his face. I felt a sense of power emanating from him and it made me nervous. Power can be dangerous if used in the wrong way. But I said nothing.

The subject was changed. 'I could send the manuscript away for typing as I usually do,' he said. 'But I may need help in sorting through documents. And then there's the child.' He broke off, and sat, deep in thought.

'The child,' I said, encouragingly.

He drew a breath. 'There are three of us

here. My cousin Alan, who manages the farm, Kitty and me. And of course, the child.'

'Has he a name?' I asked a little sharply.

'Richard. He's three. I'll take you to meet him in a moment. Kitty looks after him now.'

I was bewildered. 'But—whose child is it?' I asked. 'And what's wrong with him?'

'He's mine.' And I was shocked at the way he'd referred to his own son as "the child". But I said nothing.

'There is,' he went on, 'a weakness in his legs; he can't walk very well. Otherwise he's quite normal.'

'But—does he have treatment?' I wondered where the child was.

'He goes to a specialist once a month at the hospital in York, when Kitty manages to take him, that is. There's quite a lot to do here, with only Mrs Appleby . . . For the rest he is supposed to exercise, to be taught to walk as if he were one year old instead of three. Sometimes I think he should be sent away to a home.'

'Oh, no,' I said, appalled. 'You couldn't send your own child away. Why, he's only a baby.'

He sighed. 'Well, do you think you can cope?'

'Of course I can,' I said sturdily. 'I've studied first aid and home nursing at evening classes. I'd love to look after him.'

'Good. I thought you sounded keen in your

letter. There will be quite a lot to do. There might be days when Mrs Appleby can't get here, if the weather's bad, so you might have to turn your hand to a bit of cooking, too. Would you mind?'

'We—ell. I won't say I'm the world's best cook, but I suppose I could turn out the usual meat and two veg.'

'Good,' he said again. 'No doubt Kitty will help.'

'I assume Kitty is your wife,' I said.

'No. Kitty is Alan's mother, my aunt.'

'I see. So you have aunts, too, I can't seem to get away from them.' I wondered where Richard's mother was, and Charles seemed to divine my thought, for he said: 'I'm a widower.'

'Oh,' I said, lamely. 'I'm sorry.'

'You don't have to apologise,' he said, harshly, and I stared in surprise.

'You don't have to be sorry for me,' he went on in the same harsh tone. 'My marriage was already over.'

I flushed, I felt the colour burn my cheeks. I was angry at the way he'd snubbed me, angry with him for seeming so hard. He got up from the table saying: 'Come along.'

'Yes, Mr Blane,' I replied, wanting to retaliate. 'Or do you prefer me to call you Master Charles?' I emphasised the Master.

'Just call me Charles,' he said, indifferently. 'Mrs Appleby likes to play the old retainer, when she doesn't forget. I'll get her to take you upstairs, no need for me to go.'

Really! I thought, indignantly. As if he couldn't go to see his son . . . I didn't think I cared for my new employer at all.

Whether this showed in my face, or whether Mrs Appleby had heard our conversation I don't know, but as we reached the top of the stairs she said in a low voice. 'Don't let him upset you, Dee. He's had a deal of trouble in the past few years.'

'Well, he needn't take it out on me,' I retorted. 'Or on his little boy.'

Mrs Appleby didn't answer. She led me to the bedroom door next to mine, knocked, and went away.

*   *   *

Aunt Kitty was a plump woman, with faded blonde hair that couldn't seem to make up its mind whether it was fair or grey. She ushered me into the room then fluttered back to the armchair by the bed where the little boy lay. I said, a little uncertainly. 'You're Aunt Kitty . . . that is, I mean, Mrs Blane.'

Her fluttery manner changed, there was a hint of the grand lady as she said: 'I am the mistress of Darrenscar.' Then the hauteur disappeared and she smiled. 'But you may call me Aunt Kitty.'

'It's a nice name.' I said, a little at a loss.

'It's not my name, really. My father used to call me Kitten when I was a child, and it stuck. I was a pretty girl.'

'Yes.'

'I used to dance all night. Such fun, so many balls and parties. My parents couldn't understand why I married one of the Blanes. But they needn't have quarrelled with me as they did.' She drew her lips together.

'I'm sorry,' I said, wondering if I dare use these words again. But Aunt Kitty didn't seem to object to sympathy, seemed to welcome it, in fact.

'They were cruel to have nothing more to do with me,' she said. 'So I've been here all these years. Trapped in this house—'and I was startled again, for this was the thought I'd had when I first saw Darrenscar. *Trapped*.

I said: 'Couldn't you have moved to another place?'

'How? I had no money after my husband died. Besides, I had my son's rights to consider. Alan. You'll meet him tonight.'

'Yes,' I said.

'Alan does the farm work. In fact he does all the work while Charles just sits writing, it seems so unfair.'

I said nothing, and there was a pause. I turned towards the bed where the little boy lay, still in pyjamas. 'Hallo, Richard,' I said.

14

He was a lovely little boy, with dark hair and eyes, but his face was too pale, as if he didn't have enough fresh air. 'Doesn't he get up at all?' I asked. 'Get dressed?'

'Sometimes. But he likes to lie in bed and talk to his Auntie Kitty.'

'Isn't he supposed to exercise his legs?' I asked.

'He doesn't want to. So I don't force him.'

'Surely—' I began. 'If it would be for his own good—'

'The child needs all the love he can get,' Aunt Kitty said petulantly. 'His father doesn't care for him.'

I glanced at Richard. The child might be only three, but he looked intelligent, and it hardly seemed right to criticise his father in his presence. I moved to the side of the bed to where a large photograph stood on a little table. 'Is this Richard's mother?' I asked, cautiously.

'That's right. Marianne.'

I picked up the photograph. Marianne was dark and lovely; she was, I think, the loveliest woman I have ever seen. 'Richard isn't much like her,' I said, slowly.

'She left Charles, you know,' Aunt Kitty said. 'And who can blame her?'

I put the photograph down, saying nothing, and turned back to Richard. I wondered why his mother had left him. Did he know, and did he feel abandoned as I had when my parents

15

had died and I hadn't understood why they didn't come home? My heart went out to the quiet little boy with the white face, and I knew what I had missed in my life—there had never been anyone to love.

'You know, Richard,' I said. 'I always wished I had a little brother. Now I have you.' And he stared at me with his unwinking child's eyes.

'Why a little brother?' Aunt Kitty asked.

'I don't know.' I was unable, even if I had desired, to explain the deep need inside me, the hours I'd spent with a dream child just like this one. 'Because I was lonely, I suppose. An only child.'

'Didn't you have any friends?'

'No. Not really.' I wondered why I was confiding in Aunt Kitty, when I had never confided in my own aunt. 'No close friends. I always envied the girls who went around, arms linked, sharing each other's thoughts. I stayed apart, wishing so much to belong.'

She came towards me then, arms outstretched. 'Welcome to Darrenscar,' she said, and the grand manner was back again. She took my hands in hers, before moving to the bed to lift Richard and sit him on her lap, opening a box of chocolates.

'I think Richard needs more fresh air,' I said. 'He'll never be able to walk if he stays in bed all day.' I hoped I didn't sound interfering, but I did want to help Richard.

16

The look Aunt Kitty gave me was almost pitying. 'There is so much you don't know,' she said. 'And I have looked after Richard since he was born. Anyway, you needn't stay any longer now, I expect you'll want to unpack. I'll see you at dinner.'

'What time is dinner?' I asked, defeated.

'Seven o'clock. That's when Alan gets back. You'll meet him.'

I left the room and stood uncertainly on the landing. It didn't seem I would have the easiest of times here, between Charles Blane and Aunt Kitty. And in the middle a little boy who was, let's face it, being neglected.

Then I saw Mrs Appleby had come out of my room, and I had the feeling that she had waited for me. Her words confirmed this.

'You look fair mazed,' she said. 'Don't let her bother you, that Mrs Blane. It's just her way.'

'Her—her way?'

'Aye. The way she sometimes acts as a grand lady. It's just her way,' she repeated.

'She was talking about balls and parties she used to go to,' I said, uncertainly. 'Isn't it true?'

'Not since she came here,' Mrs Appleby said. 'Maybe she did before, I wouldn't know. It's true she came from a grand family, and ran away with Alan's father. Then her family wouldn't have any more to do with her. That's the talk, but the Blanes are not very well liked in the village. There's a good deal of bitterness.'

'Oh. Well—it's kind of you to tell me all this,' I said.

'Some of the girls we had before didn't like it, you see, when Mrs Blane starts all this "I am the mistress of Darrenscar, and you are the maid." But it's just her way. I s'pose it's a shame for her really; I mean, she doesn't have much of a life here, so she has all these dreams of the past, and being a grand lady of the manor. Pathetic, isn't it, the way Darrenscar is now? Just don't let it bother you.' And with a friendly nod Mrs Appleby trotted away, down the stairs.

But I stood, deep in thought. The whole house seemed to live in the past, what with Charles and his history, Aunt Kitty dreaming of past glories, and my feeling I'd known it all before . . .

I turned to my own room, then stopped. I walked towards the staircase where the carved wooden animals sat on each side of the balustrade. Carefully I put both hands round the first one, a squirrel, lifted it . . . it came away in my hands, as I'd known it would.

*   *   *

The bathroom was indeed new, with shining taps and blue and white tiles. The water was steaming hot, and I wallowed in a bath for a good twenty minutes. Back in my room I put on

18

my newest, prettiest dress, a pale green with full bodice and slit sleeves which brought out the reddish lights in my hair. I was wondering about Alan.

At seven o'clock I went down the stairs towards the kitchen. I could hear voices now, men's voices and squeaks from Aunt Kitty. Then the kitchen door opened and Alan stood there looking at me.

I knew him. I had always known him. This was why I'd never cared for the boys I'd met before. My love was here.

He was so handsome. His dark hair curled away from his face and fell almost to his collar. His eyes were blue. He said: 'Come, Dee,' and took both my hands in his, gently, almost caressingly. Then he led me to the table.

The atmosphere seemed lighter now. Mrs Appleby put out the meal, said Goodnight and left to get her lift. We talked, and I felt I belonged here, as I'd never belonged with Aunt Meg.

Later I was to realise that the Blanes were making a concerted effort that night to appear normal. Later I was to learn that they came together only at mealtimes, and even then bitter silences alternated with outright quarrels. But that first evening I was too dazzled by my instant love for Alan even to take much notice of what was said. Not until Alan turned to me.

'What do you think of Darrenscar?' he asked.

'I'll show you round later, outside, see the dungeon.'

I said, quickly 'I don't want to see the dungeon.'

There was a slight pause, and I felt Charles' eyes on me. But it was Alan who spoke. 'You sounded as if you knew all about it. You should have asked what dungeons are doing in a place like this?'

'And we all know the answer to that,' said Aunt Kitty.

'The dungeon was no doubt used to punish any poor soul caught stealing a sheep,' Charles put in quickly.

'Not only that,' Aunt Kitty said. 'There was the poor girl left in there to die—'

'Mother, that was a hundred years ago,' Alan interrupted. 'You're frightening Dee, see how white she's gone. Let's talk about something pleasant, like farming.'

'You don't look like a farmer,' I smiled, making an effort to overcome the sudden fear I'd felt.

'I took the straws out of my hair before I came in,' Alan laughed.

'City people have such romantic ideas of farming,' Charles commented. 'Whereas it's a business, same as any other, and not a very well-paying one when there are just sheep.'

'We could do other things,' Alan said.

'Such as?'

Alan put down his fork. 'The new road they're building, it will come right along the bottom of our land. With the road people will be able to get here from the cities. Everyone wants a country cottage these days. So we could sell land for building.'

'No,' Charles said. 'And I'll remind you, Alan, that, although you say "we", the land belongs to me.'

Alan said no more, but his face was mutinous as he drank the coffee which Aunt Kitty placed before us. Then he turned to me. 'Let's go,' he said.

We went out into the yard, and I stood, enraptured. The sun set in a blaze of orange. And immediately a great full moon rose, blood red, and the whole world was silvery blue. 'It's beautiful,' I said.

'Yes,' Alan whispered. 'And so are you.'

We walked across the yard, and I noticed that another car had been drawn up beside the Landrover and the Mini which had been there when I arrived. This was a shining, nearly new Alfa-Romeo, and I walked towards it, puzzled. 'Is this yours?' I asked, for even I, city-bred as I was, knew that you didn't need an expensive car to look after a few sheep out on the moors.

'Yes, it's mine,' Alan answered.

'So you don't only do farm work,' I said.

He laughed. 'Smart, aren't you? No, I don't, I go into York nearly every day, and if you want to know why, I might tell you later, if I can trust you to keep a secret.'

'But doesn't Charles know, and Aunt Kitty?'

'Mother lives in her own little world as you must have noticed. As for Charles, what's it to him as long as I get the farm work done as well?'

He turned away moodily and it was obvious to me now that the cousins did not get on, to put it mildly. I said, tentatively. 'Why do you stay if you don't like it? Because of your mother?'

He didn't answer for a moment. 'It's a funny set-up here,' he said, at last. 'The original Blane must have had a strange sense of humour when he ordered the estate. None of the women inherit anything, ever, and the male heirs only if they live here until they are twenty-five. So I have another three years to run.'

'Oh,' I said. 'I thought you—' I broke off, embarrassed.

'You thought we were hard up? So we are. But Charles had his inheritance, and if I lose mine it will just go back into the estate, and indirectly, to him.'

'Is it worth waiting for?' I asked, not meaning to pry, but because he seemed unhappy at Darrenscar.

He shrugged. 'Not a fortune by any means. But why turn my back on even a few thousand? I might as well take it before the whole place goes to pot. I have expensive tastes, Dee,' and he nodded towards the Alfa-Romeo.

'There seems an awful lot to cater for,' I mused. 'If the inheritance applies to all sons and cousins.'

'Oddly, no. The Blanes never did have many children. Probably because of their habit of dying violent deaths quite young. My father did, and Charles' father.'

'Well,' I commented. 'So did my parents, come to that,' but he wasn't listening.

'Maybe the gypsy's curse was right, after all,' he said.

'What was that?' I asked, startled.

'Oh, we have it all, curses, the lot. This particular little lady was dabbling in witchcraft, was put to death, but found time to curse the Blanes before she died.'

'I expect that will be part of Charles' history, and I shall type it out,' I said, trying not to shiver.

'Is that what he's doing?' Alan laughed.

'Didn't you know?'

'I'm not in Charles' confidence,' Alan said, shortly. 'But come on, enough of the Blanes.'

He steered me away from the car, around the buildings which I guessed had once been stables, and his arm was around me so that I hardly heard a word he said. Only when we came to the thick oak door let into the side of a wall next to the house did I draw back.

23

'The dungeon,' he said.

And I was filled with fear, a terrifying fear that stabbed right into me, and which I didn't understand. He opened the door and there were stone steps leading down into blackness, a deep blackness that yawned away from me into a deep pit where people could be buried alive . . . 'No,' I cried. 'I don't want to go. Don't make me . . .'

'Of course you don't have to go,' Alan said, soothingly. 'Dee, what is it? You're shivering, as if you'd seen a ghost. Don't be scared. It's not a dungeon now. It's used as a cellar. Jim Bradshaw stores the farm stuff there.' And he put his arm around me.

I stopped shivering. And when he kissed me it was as if the night was filled with music.

'Strange,' he said. 'That we've only just met. I feel as if I've known you for years.'

You, too? I asked, silently. Perhaps it was always this way when one fell in love.

He took me back to the house, and I sat dreamily till it was time to go to bed.

I lay in the darkness, realising how silent it was compared with London. No sound; you could hear the stillness. Yet it didn't seem strange in any way. London, Aunt Meg, no longer seemed part of my life. This was the reality, the other didn't matter.

*   *   *

I was happy when I woke in the morning, and my happiness continued even though Alan had already left when I went down. Charles seemed in a pleasant mood. He told me he'd like me to work with him in the mornings, then help with Richard in the afternoons. Everything was going to be all right, I told myself. I would speak to Charles about Richard, see the doctor if necessary. Meanwhile I followed Charles into the study.

It was a fairly large room, with oak panelled walls, two of them lined with books. The one small window did not give clear views of the moors, as at the back, but of the trees surrounding the side and front of the house, and which had no doubt been planted as a windbreak. This, I thought, had once been used as the schoolroom . . . hadn't it? I sat at my typewriter, eager to begin.

But Charles seemed to hesitate, he fumbled with the papers, walked to the window and came back. At last he sat down.

'Dee,' he said. 'Before we begin, there is something I have to say.'

'Yes?' I wondered if I'd done something wrong.

'You asked me why I was writing this history. Well, to answer that I must start at the beginning. I didn't go to university; when I was eighteen I trained as a journalist on a paper in a

25

nearby town. This did two things for me, it made me cynical, and gave me a nose for news.'

He paused, but I did not interrupt.

'Five years ago I came into my inheritance. I had already started writing my books, so I decided to stay at home. Unfortunately I hadn't realised how badly Darrenscar was in need of repair. I had the whole place modernised, and we found everything was rotting, dry rot, wet rot, woodworm, we had the lot. So that took care of my inheritance, and as I'd given up my job I had to work hard. I was married then.'

I wondered if he was going to tell me about Marianne, but he did not.

'I knew the general outline of the history of Darrenscar, naturally, though not a lot, for my parents died when I was very young, Alan's father, too. Then—something happened a few years ago—' he broke off, and again I felt that he was assessing me in some way.

I said: 'Something happened—?' but he did not explain. He went on. 'I started going through the documents, trying to—understand. That's why I want it all typed out clearly, so that I can study everything, find out . . .'

Again a pause. 'Find out?' I encouraged.

'You seem to think I was a little hard on my ancestor. Geoffrey Blane, who built this house. Not so. By all accounts he was a wicked man.'

'But that was a long time ago,' I said.

'His influence lingers. First of all, the estate,

that all male heirs lived here until twenty-five.'

'Alan told me about that,' I said. 'But surely there's no harm—'

'Except that it meant that two or three brothers or cousins, usually only two, oddly, were forced to be together at an age when young men are too often aggressive, in an isolated spot with few women—'

'Ah.'

'I see you draw the inevitable conclusion. And then there was the gipsy girl.'

'Who cursed you. Alan mentioned that, too. But surely you don't believe in such things?'

'I don't know. One tends to laugh, I did at first, until—' again he broke off.

I felt a touch of apprehension, unease at the knowledge that was to be given to me, that I could not escape.

'Geoffrey Blane brought the gipsy girl here into Darrenscar, into his bed, and that of his brother, too. You will read the full story if you decide to stay. Briefly, the girl was accused of witchcraft.'

'By whom?'

'By the villagers, at first.'

'Oh, Charles, superstitious peasants!'

He shrugged. 'It was Geoffrey Blane who threw her into the dungeon, and then reported her to the magistrates. She was tried as a witch, and hanged. But before she died she shouted: "You will come back in every century, Blane, and when you and your brother are together then I will be there and if I am a witch then I can cause possession by evil spirits from the Devil my master. Neither you nor your brother will have any other light of love. They will die, and you will suffer for it."'

I was silent, and outside the trees rustled although there was no wind. I wanted to mock this as rubbish, but something deep inside me was scared.

Charles said: 'Dee, do you believe in reincarnation?'

Now I looked up, startled. 'I don't know much about it,' I said. 'People having lived before, you mean?

'Yes, there has been much talk about it recently, about people who have been taken back by hypnotism till they remember other lives . . . someone said that if you go to a place and feel you have been there before, it means you really have. If you feel you've met a person before, then you have, in another life . . .'

My heart was beginning to beat heavily, I had a strange sensation in my ears . . .

'Going through the Darrenscar papers,' Charles' voice went on remorselessly, 'I've seen the same pattern repeating itself several times.'

My heart was pounding now. 'You mean the gipsy's curse?'

'I mean that, in the past, once in every century only, have there been two Blane men

28

living in the house, brothers or cousins, and in those times there was a girl—'

'Yes?'

'She was always a stranger who came to the house. She became entangled with one or other of the men—or both.'

'I—I see.'

'And,' he added flatly, 'she was killed, I think murdered, probably by one of the Blanes. Now, Dee, do you still want to stay?'

CHAPTER TWO

A hundred thoughts chased through my mind in the few minutes I sat watching Charles Blane. *If you go to a place and feel you've been there before, it means you really have. If you feel you've met a person before, then you have, in another life* . . . I looked through the window. The trees stood tall and aloof, and I wondered how long they had been there, what they had seen. Then I heard my voice, strange and flat, saying: 'But you don't believe this?'

'I don't know. It seems odd, that's all. I thought you should know, and then decide if you will stay.'

I thought fleetingly of Alan, my new-found love. What had I felt when we met? I know him, I've always known him . . . If we parted,

29

wouldn't we just meet again somewhere, sometime . . .

I said, carefully. 'This pattern you mention. Can you explain it more fully?'

He doodled with a pen on his blotter. 'Well, first there was Geoffrey Blane and the gipsy, in Sixteen seventy-nine. When she was in the dungeon he took another girl, Jane Webber, who died. In Seventeen-eighty there was a serving-maid run down by an unknown horseman, and in Eighteen eighty-three a governess, who died in strange circumstances. I thought maybe the people had to keep reappearing until the problem was worked out satisfactorily.'

'You mean until the gipsy's curse was conquered?'

'Yes. Or until it won. You see, although those lights of love seem to have been murdered, no Blane was ever made to suffer for the crime.'

'And you think it's happening again, this pattern? Now? That would mean that you are one of the protagonists.' I wanted to ask him if he *knew* he was, but didn't quite dare. I was afraid of his answer.

He said: 'Alan, too.'

'It sounds incredible. I just can't see—' I was stalling for time, trying to work out what it meant for me . . . If I told Charles of my feelings since I'd been here would he tell me to go? Or, as seemed more likely, leave me to choose, work out my own destiny? Pretty poor destiny it would be if I were murdered.

'Tell me about the last time,' I said.

'Well . . . a hundred years ago my great grandfather, Stephen Blane, lived here with his wife and children, and his younger brother, Robert. They engaged a young governess for the children, a stranger, an orphan, Mary Dean.'

I felt cold and didn't know why. I asked. 'Yes?'

'She wrote a diary, you can read it later. She was in love with Robert, and found she was pregnant, a pretty serious thing in those days. But the family allowed her to stay, the diary records her feelings right up to the last month. Then—she was found dead, in the dungeon, with the newly-born child, also dead, and also named Richard. That's all we know.'

'Was there an inquest?'

'Of course. The verdict was accidental death.'

'Then why suspect murder?'

'Just rumours, I suppose. The village firmly believes it was murder, to this day. But you can read the diary, judge for yourself.'

'But what about your father, and Alan's? They were brothers, were they not?'

'Yes, but oddly, they were never together, as adults. My father was in the war, and stayed in the Army of occupation, was killed abroad by

31

an unexploded bomb in Nineteen fifty-one. Alan's father married Aunt Kitty the year before, died in a car crash when Alan was very small. My family do seem to go in for violent deaths one way and another.'

'Well,' I said, with a confidence I did not feel, 'it rests with me, doesn't it? Not to get entangled with the Blane men?' I thought of Alan, and wondered if it was not already too late.

'Destiny works in strange ways,' said Charles. 'Sometimes I think that it's something in the house itself, some evil, if you like, striving for mastery, perhaps an unquiet spirit seeking possession—' he broke off, and his eyes were dark and brooding.

I didn't understand what he meant—not then. I wondered if he were mad, and felt a stirring of fear. He said: 'I suppose I should have told you all this before you came.'

'Why didn't you?'

'I must admit I was pretty desperate for help. Not for the typing, but for the child. Aunt Kitty just can't cope with a three-year-old boy.'

'You've had help before,' I stated.

'Several girls. But they never stay.'

'Why not?' I was feeling cold again.

'I don't really know, except that it's so lonely here. I've never told them about this theory of mine.'

'Why not?' I repeated.

32

He shrugged. 'It just didn't seem relevant.'

'And it seems relevant to tell me?' *Why me?*

He stared at me strangely. 'It just didn't seem fair somehow, not to tell you.'

'Were there many applications?' I asked.

'Only yours.'

'And if I don't stay?'

'Then Richard will have to go into a home. Maybe that will be the best thing for him.'

That decided me. I could leave Alan, and we could arrange to meet again. But I couldn't leave the child who meant so much to me, the little brother I'd always wanted, the child who filled a gap in my love-starved life.

'I love Richard,' I said, softly. 'I'll stay.'

'Good,' he said. 'I hoped you would. Well, you needn't do any typing now, I'll get things ready for tomorrow. It will sooon be lunch time, so run along, perhaps you can give Mrs Appleby a hand.'

I stood up. 'There is one thing—'

'Yes?'

'About Richard. Am I to have a free hand?'

'Of course.' He sat back, putting down his pen.

'I'd like,' I said, boldly, 'to see the doctor myself, listen to his diagnosis and carry out his instructions.'

'As you wish. I think the child is due for his treatment in a few days. Perhaps you can take him into York. You do drive?'

'Yes.' I hadn't a car, but had taken driving lessons. 'I don't think,' I went on, hesitantly, 'that Aunt Kitty will like it. She seems to want to be in charge herself.'

'I'll speak to her. Don't worry about it.' He sounded bored, and I wished he could take a real interest in Richard. He had engaged me to look after him much as one would care for a sick animal, I thought resentfully. There was no love.

But there seemed nothing more to say, so I went into the kitchen.

*　　*　　*

It was so bright and sunny in here that the conversation in the study seemed part of a dream. Darrenscar might be old and gloomy at the front, but the kitchen was pleasant and light, the blue plates shining, the wide window giving an uninterrupted view. Even today, when I am so far away, I can still see the moors in all their beauty, remember the changing colours and shadows as the sun moved, turning the bracken to golden brown, the heather to purple, the far hills sometimes blue, sometimes black. And over all the great sky. 'It's so lovely,' I said.

'Aye,' said Mrs Appleby. 'It is in the summer. And we're having a fine autumn. But it's bad in the winter, and old Jim Bates down

34

in the village says we're in for a real bad one. He always reckons to tell the weather.'

'And is he correct?'

'Usually he is.'

'Well, it's pleasant enough now. I haven't seen the village yet. There's no sign of it from here.'

'No. It's down in the valley. But only a couple of miles.'

'Incredible,' I said.

'Aye. It's all right for them as likes it.' I gave a questioning glance, and Mrs Appleby went on. 'What I mean is, most people take comfort from the sight of another human house.'

'Yes, I suppose you're right,' I agreed.

'All right if you can stand it.'

'Being isolated?'

'It's not that.' Mrs Appleby put a saucepan on the cooker. 'But when several people are stuck together and there doesn't seem to be anybody else in the world, that can mean trouble.'

'Yes.' Hadn't Charles said the same thing, about the family being forced to live together? Mrs Appleby brought a new dimension, the feeling of being alone in the world. I turned from the window. 'Is there anything I can do to help?'

'Aye, you can lay the table, if you will. Take the blue plates from the dresser. Knives and forks are in the drawer.'

I set to work. 'How many will there be?' I asked.

'Three, with you, maybe two, you'd better ask. The little boy always eats in his room.'

'Surely that's wrong,' I said, quickly. 'He's shut away like a prisoner. He should be here, with the family. I must tell Aunt Kitty.'

'Aye, well, Master Charles didn't really want the boy downstairs. There's times he couldn't bear to see him.'

I stopped my work. 'Why should he take against his own son?'

Mrs Appleby, usually the soul of honesty, seemed evasive. 'He has his reasons, I suppose.'

I wondered if he was so much in love with Marianne that he couldn't bear to see the child who reminded him of her. Was that the reason, or was it that Charles Blane was a cold, hard sort of person? Was that why Marianne left him?

I said, 'Alan won't be back yet.'

'No, he don't come till night.'

I wanted to talk about Alan; I'd have been happy just to keep repeating his name. 'The farm—' I began, and remembered he'd told me he went into York every day. But Mrs Appleby was unperturbed.

'He's not very interested in farming,' she said.

'Why do it then?' I asked.

'He went to college, failed his exams the first

year, got badly into debt, I believe, and so came home. Course, he had to come here because of the will. So Charles gave him the farm work. But he don't bother with it. Leaves it all to Jim Bradshaw, while he's off to town. And that don't please Jim Bradshaw none, either.'

I wondered why this news didn't shake my feeling for Alan, but in fact I felt sorry for him, forced back to Darrenscar, forced into farming . . . 'Why should Charles do this?' I asked, angrily.

'Well, Alan had to live here, that's the way the estate's ordered, and the oldest son is responsible for the other members of the family.'

I might have known Charles wouldn't do anything out of kindness. He was forced to, under the estate. 'And doesn't that apply to his son?' I asked. 'When he talks of putting him in a home?'

'Mebbe so,' said Mrs Appleby a little warily. 'But if he were in a home Charles' ud have to pay, he'd still be responsible, wouldn't he? Now, run upstairs and tell Mrs Blane the lunch is ready. And I'll tell the Master—we've been chattering long enough.' And with this reproof she moved away.

⋆　　　⋆　　　⋆

I walked slowly upstairs to Richard's room.

37

Lunch was over, and I'd helped Mrs Appleby with the washing up. I thought of the empty rooms that must have been in use when the governess was here, and promised myself I'd look through them when I had the chance. But for the moment there was Richard . . . I entered his room, and he was in bed, as yesterday, with Aunt Kitty knitting in her rocking chair.

'Time to dress Richard, Aunt Kitty,' I said, brightly.

She did not answer, but began counting stitches.

'Aunt Kitty.' If a stand had to be made, then it must be made now. 'I am to look after Richard, his father has told me. I am to be in charge.'

I thought she would argue, but she did not. Her head drooped as she said: 'Aunt Kitty's the one who always stays.'

'I shall stay,' I said. 'I like this house.'

'I hate it,' Aunt Kitty's usually placid voice was bitter. 'I'd sell my soul to get away.'

I looked at her, fair and faded, and knew a sudden sympathy. 'Can't Alan do something for you?' I asked.

'He can't leave, or Charles would take Darrenscar. That's what he'd like. I'm trapped here. But when we have money again it will be like the old days.'

'Yes,' I said, a little bored.

'It was so wonderful,' Aunt Kitty said. 'Carriages driving up to the door, ladies in their fine clothes and jewels. Such marvellous balls.'

'Ye—es,' I murmured. So this was what Mrs Appleby had meant when she talked about Aunt Kitty living in the past. I looked at her fully again, and the petulant droop had left her face, her head was up high, proudly, as if she were indeed the lady of Darrenscar, receiving her guests.

I shivered. It was a little uncanny. Yet when I looked at her again she was the faded petulant woman she'd been before.

I turned back to Richard. What effect would all this have on the child? To be alone with a woman who lived in the past? I said, firmly: 'Aunt Kitty, we'll have to work this out. I have to look after Richard, that's my job. I want to give him exercise, help him to walk. I hope to persuade Charles to let him come downstairs more often. But in the meantime I am paid to look after him.'

'Like a governess,' said Aunt Kitty.

Again I looked at her, but her eyes were guileless. 'Yes,' I said, flatly, 'like a governess. And I shall take him to see the doctor in York. When is the next appointment?'

'I don't know.' Slowly she got to her feet, and I wondered if I were being unkind. After all, if she loved the child . . . But love that smothered could do no good, and Richard's welfare came first. 'I'll look for it,' she said, and went out.

She did not come back, so I stayed with Richard. 'Now,' I began. 'My name is Dee.'

He stared, but said nothing. 'You're too serious,' I said, 'and small wonder. Say Dee.' I tickled him, and he gave a chuckle, then he was laughing. 'Dee,' he shouted. 'Dee-Dee. Dee-Dee.' And I was Dee-Dee from that moment.

It was a happy afternoon. I washed and dressed him, talked to him, tried to help him take a few stumbling steps, and all the time I felt my love for him strengthen. What did I care for silly rumours about murdered governesses a hundred years ago? I had Richard, and in the evening there would be Alan.

I felt that Richard liked me, too, he seemed to respond to my care, laughed with glee when I teased him, listened while I told him a little story. I asked him if he had any books. He stared, blankly.

I searched in the cupboards, the drawers, and he watched me silently. He would always retreat into silence, I was to learn, if there was something he did not understand. But in the room I did not find a single book, and no toys.

I was shocked beyond belief. Even in orphanages children had toys. 'When we go into York,' I said. 'I'll buy you some presents.'

Aunt Kitty came back about four, with tea, and she said: 'I've found the appointment card, and it's for tomorrow.'

'Tomorrow?' That was soon, but maybe it was all the better. 'Thank you, Aunt Kitty,' I said. 'You're very kind. Will you stay with Richard while I go down for tea?'

I felt it was the least I could do.

*　　*　　*

I left the room but I did not go straight into the kitchen, I wanted to explore the shut up rooms at the front of Darrenscar. So I slipped along the passage and opened the first door.

This was the dining room, with a long table and chairs along the centre. I could not see much more for the heavy curtains were drawn. Once, I thought, the Blanes ate here, while the governess, poor Mary Dean, had a tray in her room. Neither servant nor family, but one who wanted desperately to belong, just as I did . . .

I closed the door quietly, and went to the drawing room, where the old faded chairs were covered with dust sheets. A heavy musty smell hung over everything; in one dark corner I could see cobwebs. Here, the lady of the house would receive her guests, sometimes the children would be brought in by Mary Dean, who sat quietly in a corner, alone . . .

The last room was large, running all along the front and side of the house. The ballroom. I tiptoed to one of the big windows and pulled

41

the curtains back a few inches, letting a beam of light shine through the dust and emptiness. In one corner, almost hidden, was a tiny staircase, and I climbed up to an equally tiny balcony. I looked down. There the jewelled ladies and their well-dressed escorts would dance, coming from miles around for the house parties for which Darrenscar was famous. And here, in the balcony, Mary Dean, the governess, would gaze down at the fashionable throng. Which of them had taken her to the dungeon to die? Did she know?

I crept down the stairs again, but before I closed the curtains peeped out at the lonely moors stretching it seemed to infinity. What long journeys they must have had in their carriages, those people of long ago, and how uncomfortable, jolting over the rough roads.

I ran upstairs, looking at the closed doors of the bedrooms. Then, daringly, I opened them all. The three occupied ones I left hastily, but in the others I lingered. There was the same musty smell, the same uncared for look, though several of them had modern furniture, had no doubt been used by Charles' and Alan's parents.

But the main front bedroom was different. Over the ballroom, it was much bigger, and in its centre was a huge four-poster bed that looked as though it had stood there for centuries. The room was crowded with old, massive furniture, perhaps brought in from other rooms. I went towards a great oak chest, opened it, and saw that it was full of clothes, and on the top was a green velvet gown.

I lifted it out, held it up. Extremely elaborate, it had frills, ruchings, and a sort of train that spread from the waist to the floor. The round *decolletée* was very deep indeed. I wondered, as I folded it carefully, who it had belonged to? I replaced it in the chest, gave a last look at the huge four-poster, then slipped away.

All the bedrooms were large, even Richard's. A sudden thought struck me, and I ran to my own room at the end. The smallest of all. The governess's room. This must have belonged to Mary Dean.

★ ★ ★

At dinner that evening I heard the first of the family squabbles, and learned of the hot tempers of the Blane men. I'm not sure how it started. I had been sitting quietly next to Alan, happy to be near him, wondering what it must have been like to work in the kitchen in the old days, without all the mod. cons. I heard Charles say 'Alan,' harshly, and I jumped out of my reverie.

'I've had some bills today,' Charles went on. 'Your bills, charged to my name.'

43

'I thought it could come out of the estate,' Alan said easily.

'There's not a lot to come out of the estate,' Charles retorted.

'Oh well then, I'll pay,' Alan said.

'Can you pay?'

'Well, later perhaps.'

'You never pay,' Charles said, cuttingly. 'You're paid for the farm work you don't do, and I can't have you running up more bills.'

'Can I help it if we have to live like paupers?' Now Alan was angry.

'It's you who keep us paupers,' Charles shouted.

'I wish we could sell the place,' Alan said sullenly.

'So do I. But I can't, and you know that, too.'

'Of course it must not be sold,' Aunt Kitty put in. 'Not Darrenscar.'

'No, Mother,' said Alan, patiently.

'If Charles doesn't want the house, then it will come to you, Alan,' Aunt Kitty went on.

'You're forgetting Richard,' Charles said, and I sensed malice in his tone. There was a sudden pause, then they started again.

'You could sell the land, as I told you yesterday,' Alan said.

'I can't. Everything's tied up—'

'By our ancestors who wanted us to live as a happy family,' mocked Alan. 'But you're

44

wrong, Charles. That land by the road was added later. You could sell it. Building a few houses would mean everything to us.'

'I'm not sure that I want to have rows of holiday bungalows near my back door,' said Charles.

'Back door my foot! They wouldn't be as close as all that,' Alan retorted.

'And we could live as we used to do,' said Aunt Kitty, dreamily. 'I didn't think, when I married your father, Alan, that I'd be reduced to this—' and she flung out her arm, dramatically.

I sat silent. At first I'd been a little embarrassed, wondering why they discussed their business affairs before me, a stranger. And then realisation hit me. I was like Mary Dean, just a governess, not worth bothering about. The knowledge annoyed me, and I said. 'How did the Blanes lose their money?'

If I'd thought I'd shock them I was wrong. Alan smiled. 'A good question,' he said, but Charles answered seriously. 'They had a lot of foreign investments, which they lost after the war,' he told me. 'As for the rest, they were always an extravagant lot.'

'Like me,' said Alan, with his sweet smile, and as I rose to pass around the apple pie, he caught my hand. 'I'm going to take you into York one of these days,' he said.

'I'm going tomorrow,' I told him. 'To take

Richard to hospital. That is—' I looked at Charles, 'if I may take the car?'

He nodded, and Alan said. 'Then we'll meet. Do you know York at all?'

'No.'

'Well, there's a car park here.' He scribbled a little map on an envelope and passed it to me. 'What time? Five-ish?'

'I'm not sure if it's wise,' Aunt Kitty said.

I was startled. Alan said, warningly. 'Now, Mother—' but she went on: 'Remember what happened before, when the son of the house mixed with the governess. It isn't wise.'

I gaped, and then I was angry. I saw Charles shake his head but I couldn't hold back my temper. 'I've never met such ill-mannered people in my life,' I said. 'No wonder you can't keep girls here.' And I marched from the room, and upstairs.

I half hoped Alan would come after me, but he did not. No one came. I went to the window of my little room and gazed out. There was no moon tonight, it was quite dark. A rising wind moaned over the moors. The Indian summer was over.

★   ★   ★

I regretted my temper in the morning. I tried to excuse Aunt Kitty, she was a pathetic old woman, living in dreams, but her words had hurt. They somehow brought my shining love down to the level of a cheap little affair. Alan amusing himself with the maid, and it was this I resented. But no one referred to my hasty words and when breakfast was over I went into the study with Charles.

He handed me some of the papers. 'This is the beginning,' he said. 'Can you read my writing?'

I riffled through the pages, stopping at number four, for this was different. Written on old paper, it seemed to be an account of the gipsy girl at Darrenscar. I saw that Charles was waiting for my answer, so I said, hurriedly: 'Yes, I can read it, thanks.'

'Good,' he said. 'I'll leave you to it, then. Everything's there, paper, carbons, and I'll have two copies please. Be back soon.' And he was gone.

Alone, I turned to the paper, and began to read.

'*In the reign of King Charles II, 1679*

'*As concerning the Gipsy. She came to Darrenscar to work in the kitchen. It is said that both the Blane men lay with her, and that Geoffrey Blane sent away his wife and took the gipsy to his bed.*

'*Then the serving-maids began to complain in the village about the practices that went on at Darrenscar. The gipsy was a witch, they said, and Geoffrey Blane helped her in her rites. They saw him kill a black cockerel and drink the blood, saw him and the gipsy naked on the grass, coupling, when the moon was full. A deputation went up from the village to see Geoffrey Blane, saying that these things were not fit for decent Christian maids to see, and that the gipsy was a witch. Geoffrey laughed loud and said he was tired of the wench and threw her into the dungeon, taking Jane Webber, another serving-maid, to his bed.*

'Then strange afflictions came to Darrenscar, cattle and sheep sickened and died, and Jane Webber died of a fever. Geoffrey Blane reported the gipsy to the magistrates as a witch. She refused to confess to witchcraft, or being in league with the Devil, even after having been trussed and thrown into a pond, kept awake for three nights, and being placed in the stocks. But the justices took heed of Geoffrey Blane's evidence, and that of his brother, James, and his ten-year-old son, and the gipsy was hanged.

'Before she died she screamed out: "I will get my revenge, Blane, for what you have done to me. I was an honest maid once, but you made me your harlot, though you promised to wed me. You will come back, in every century, Blane, and when you and your brother are together then I will be there. I will get what I want. If I am a witch then I can cause possession by evil spirits from the Devil my master. Neither you nor your brother will have any other light of love, they will die and *you* will

suffer. This is my curse, Blane, and only one thing will conquer it, and that you will never know".

'*Then she died, and the crowd roared, but Geoffrey Blane asked that her body might not be burnt, but that he could have it and take it away for disposal. This was granted.*'

I sat for a long time after reading this. I felt shocked, degraded even by the narrative. The words had seared into my brain and I felt I would never get them out. I thought of the gipsy girl here . . . in the bed, that four-poster I had been looking at . . . all around the house . . .

I don't know how long I sat there. When Charles came in I looked up, helplessly.

'What is it?' he asked.

'It's—this.'

'Has it upset you? Well, don't let it. That was a brutal age, you know.'

I said, simply. 'I'm afraid.'

'Why, Dee? Look, if you'd rather not type it, I'll send it out.'

'No,' I said. 'I want to type it. I want to know about Mary Dean.'

'The governess?'

'Why should she have to suffer because of this?'

'People do suffer,' he said, soberly. 'Maybe we shouldn't blame curses, maybe it's the easy way out. Maybe the fault is not in our stars, but in ourselves.'

I looked fully at him then, and I knew he had been hurt. I knew because I had been hurt, when my parents died and I hadn't understood, and Aunt Meg didn't want me. I said: 'It's a terrible thing, to be rejected.'

'Yes.' And I saw the pain on his face.

I wanted to change the subject. 'Why don't you sell that land for building?' I asked. 'Do you think it would spoil the area?'

'It wouldn't do that, it's in a hollow. No, it's because I can't bear people. I know we need the money, but I couldn't—'

I had to turn away from the naked pain on his face.

I looked again at the record of the gipsy. 'This curse,' I said. 'And the pattern that emerged, how could it affect you?'

'Because—if there is such a thing as reincarnation, and I am a reincarnation of Stephen—'

'Yes?'

'And if Stephen killed Mary Dean—'

'And was not punished, so the pattern goes on.' I was scared suddenly. 'But this is nonsense, Charles. Just because your ancestors were wicked doesn't mean that you—'

'I nearly killed a man once,' he said, his voice trembling.

'Oh, my God.' I was cold, shivering. 'But you didn't—?'

'Only because someone stopped me.'

'And you think—' I swallowed. 'You think you didn't do it of your own free will? That you were *possessed*?'

'The gipsy did say she would call on evil spirits to take possession of others,' said Charles. 'That's why I must know what happened in the past. The earlier cases have left little trace. Mary Dean is the first to leave a diary, and even that is inconclusive. She may well have committed suicide.'

'But you don't believe that, do you?' I asked.

'No,' he said. 'She was murdered.'

'What happened to the gipsy's body when Geoffrey Blane took it away?' I asked.

'I haven't been able to find that out.'

'Shouldn't she have been buried at the crossroads with a stake through her heart? To prevent her lingering around here, calling on evil spirits to possess others?'

'Yes, but she wasn't. So we have to look for the one thing which will break the curse, as she said—'

'Only one thing will conquer it, and that you will never know,' I quoted.

'That was said to Geoffrey, something he'd never know.'

'Then,' I tried to speak lightly, 'let's hope we'll be more successful.' And I returned to the typing.

Charles seemed his normal self at lunch, and afterwards carried Richard down to the Mini, and gave me full instructions on how to get to the hospital. 'Will you manage?' he asked.

'I'll be fine.'

He hesitated. 'You are going to see Alan?'

'I am. Have you any objections?'

'Don't be so touchy, Dee. I just wondered if it was wise?'

'Don't worry,' I said. 'I'm not going to play the harlot. That's the expression, isn't it? That would put me next in line for—' I broke off at the look of sheer horror on his face. 'I—I'm sorry,' I stammered.

He said: 'You will treat what I told you in confidence?'

'Of course.' And I drove away.

It was a relief to be away from Darrenscar. The sun did not shine today, but it was clear, with a nip in the air that betokened how soon it would be November. I drove along the single track road that led from the village to the main road, turned right and carried on. I took one fleeting glance behind me as I drove, Darrenscar was lost to sight, it was as if it did not exist.

I felt as though I'd just come out of prison, was in another world. I let the window down slightly and drew in deep breaths of the moorland air. It was like wine. 'All right, Richard?' I called. 'I'm going to buy you some toys today, we're going to have a lovely time.'

And I'm going to see Alan, my heart sang.

I drove through charming little villages, past small farmsteads and historic castles that had stood brooding for centuries. I was away from the moors now, into lush countryside, heading towards the city that exercised a power of attraction towards strangers because of its aura of past glories. York, one time capital of England, one time capital of a Viking kingdom, once a Roman settlement, founded, according to legend when King David ruled in Judaea, three thousand years ago. Had Mary Dean walked through its streets then?

It was strange to be in the bustle of a city after the loneliness of Darrenscar, but I found the hospital without much difficulty, and we were taken through to Dr Rowlands, the paediatrician, who, while Richard was taken by a nurse for his special massage and exercises, was quite willing to answer my questions.

His words were cheering. There was still weakness in the boy's legs, but, given the right care, there was no reason why he should not be perfectly normal in time. Asked about his staying in bed, I was told he must get up, must exercise his legs, must be helped to walk, though not allowed to get overtired.

'The child is not an invalid,' the doctor said.

'He is a perfectly healthy boy apart from this weakness which can be put right.'

'I see. Thank you,' I said. *And when I get back Charles will know this, too. No more pushing the boy out of sight.*

I turned to the door. 'By the way,' Dr Rowlands had said. 'Don't worry if you can't bring him every month. Just keep on with the treatment at home.'

'But I shall bring him every month,' I said, surprised.

'I doubt if you will in winter,' the doctor said. 'You are living in a very remote place. Many a winter Darrenscar gets snowed up, and apart from that, when the roads are icy, it's hardly wise to travel unnecessarily.'

I stared, astonished. London-bred, I had no idea there were parts of the country where it was impossible to travel in winter. Yet Mrs Appleby had warned me, too.

I shivered a little as I collected Richard. I didn't really relish the thought of being cooped up in Darrenscar. But my mood of trepidation disappeared as I put Richard in his little push-cart and set off for the shops, and his eyes grew round with wonder as we toured the toy department of a big store. I spent recklessly, buying picture-books, tiny motor cars, a small railway engine, and building bricks.

I asked the assistant if there was anything I could get to help him walk, and she showed me a wooden horse on wheels, a big engine to be pushed along. 'Which would your little boy like?' she asked.

I laughed 'Oh, he isn't my little boy. I'm just looking after him.'

'Well now,' the girl said. 'And I thought he looked like you.'

It pleased me, somehow, to be mistaken for Richard's mother.

Richard settled for the engine, and we made our way out of the store. I managed to get the packages back to the car, piled them in the back, then, breathless, sat and waited for Alan.

He was on time. 'Dee,' he cried, joyously. 'Lovely to see you. There's a little restaurant near here, shall we eat?'

'Love to,' I said.

'I can't spare much time, must get back to the office,' he said as we sat down, and he ordered. 'We must come out one evening, Dee. What do you say?'

'I'd like that, Alan' And my heart was singing again.

'Only—' he was toying with his fork. 'I think maybe it would be better if we kept it to ourselves.'

My head jerked up. 'You mean because of your mother?'

'There's no point in making trouble, Dee. It will only upset her.'

'Why should it?' And as he didn't answer. 'I

55

was annoyed at what she said last night, Alan.'

'You have to make allowances, Dee. She doesn't mean anything personally. She just wanders off like that. It's her age, I suppose.'

'But she can't be all that old?'

'In her fifties, I think. She married young, but I wasn't born for some years.'

I was silent, and he went on. 'You see, she did come from a wealthy home. Her parents disowned her in true melodramatic manner, so I suppose she takes refuge in dreaming of the past. Life here has been a constant grind.'

'You don't think she's going back into another life?'

Alan laughed. 'Good lord, no. What weird ideas you do have, Dee! Lots of people dream about the past, half England I should imagine.'

'Charles believes these things,' I said, stubbornly.

'Oh well, he would. He lives in the past, too, with his histories. Not me, I live in the present.'

'Strange,' I mused.

'What's strange about living in the present?'

'Nothing.' But I was disappointed. I had wanted to talk to him about my thoughts, my fears, but knew I could not. He wouldn't understand. So what about Charles' theory that Alan had lived before? Either he was wrong, or Alan didn't know it.

I looked round the restaurant, the smiling ordinary people, talking and laughing. It was a million miles from Darrenscar, and I knew I must keep in touch with this real world, must come here as often as I could. So I said: 'I'll meet you again, Alan.'

'That's my sweetheart. And not a word to anyone?'

'I suppose not. You're very much under your mother's influence, aren't you, Alan?'

'Am I?' He shrugged. 'Most fellows are fond of their mothers, I suppose.'

'Yes.' But that wasn't quite what I'd meant.

We went back to the car-park, and he left me. I watched him walk away, loving him, yet somehow disappointed. I did not want to meet in secret, didn't see the need for it. I wondered if he took many girls out. Of course he would, he was the type who liked girls, and girls liked him. But I loved him.

We were caught up in the rush hour traffic and this made us late getting out of York. I hoped Richard would not be tired, but he could sleep in the car. I thought with pleasure of the gifts he had. I must try to make Charles understand how wrong it was to neglect the child in this way. So Charles had been hurt, and was no doubt in retreat from the world, but surely he could spare a little love for his son?

I was clear of York now, going north. A mist swirled around the road, slowing me up further. As I approached Darrenscar the mist had cleared, the moon scudded out fitfully from between tufts of cloud. There was little traffic around now, the moors were black.

I was on the last lap, going up the hill. I came to the top and could see the black shadow that was Darrenscar, with the tall trees around it, no lights at the front, but something shining faintly from the side. And a strange feeling came over me, almost a sort of dread that I could not explain.

★   ★   ★

That night I had a terrifying dream. I was lying in the dungeon, in the blackness, I was cold and very frightened, for I knew I was going to die. I had a baby in my arm, I knew it was a baby though I couldn't see it. Then I moved my arm and the baby was Richard, the three-year-old Richard I knew. I woke, sweating and gasping, and jumped out of bed to the window to gulp in some air.

It was very dark outside. There was no moon now, no light anywhere. Nothing but blackness, black as a tomb, or a dungeon.

CHAPTER THREE

There had been days in October when the mists swirled round the tops of the hills like wraiths and were swept away by the sun. In November a real fog developed, the moors were blotted out to nothingness, Darrenscar was alone in a cotton wool world. I sat alone in the study, an old, leather bound volume before me, and picked out the faded letters on the cover. Mary Dean. Her Journal.

For four weeks I had typed feverishly every morning, tracing the history of Darrenscar and the rowdy, roistering Blanes, their wives and mistresses.

The first Blane, I gathered, made his fortune by floating false companies in England's increasing trade, and his descendants swelled the coffers, dealing in the slave trade, at home and abroad, shipping negroes to America, and transporting pauper children from London workhouses to work in the northern cotton mills. The Blanes spent long periods in London, in gaming houses, and, if accompanied by their wives, at house-parties, always on the fringes of the best society, never quite inside it.

The Stuarts gave way to the Hanoverians, just as profligate, but not so hard on witches, and there were no more witch-hangings. Yet in country places, such as Darrenscar, old beliefs die hard, and there was much village lore of hobgoblins being seen in the neighbourhood, scraps of writing from here and there, put together from an age when the ordinary men and women were illiterate.

It was perfectly true that, although sons were born to the Blanes, it was not until Seventeen-eighty that two brothers again grew to manhood, Jonathan and Randolf. A pauper child, Sarah Robinson was brought to work in the kitchen of Darrenscar before they married their wives. *'An industrious maid, very fair of face,'* it was not difficult to understand how it was that soon she was sitting at table with her two masters, sharing their lives. Nothing more was said until her death: *'The maid was found near the village, run down by an unknown horseman, left dead.'* Questioned, the villagers who witnessed the accident, spoke of a tall figure on a black horse, wearing a long cloak and a wide-brimmed hat, face covered by a mask. One of the Blanes? Questioned further, the villagers grew more hesitant, and it was obvious that by the time the enquiry was over, the horseman had entered village annals as a ghost rider, the Devil on horseback.

Another century, and the Blanes bought railway shares, home and abroad. Victoria was on the throne, and England became respectable, at least on the surface. Mary Dean came to Darrenscar, governess to the two children of Stephen Blane, the first of the lights of love to write her own story, and it was here, before me. With trembling hands I opened the pages and began to read the thin, faded, writing, hoping I might learn the truth.

January 1st, 1883

'Robert came to my room last night. I have been so happy these past few weeks. With the guests here for Christmas—and still here—I was allowed to join in the festivities, though I fear Mr Stephen Blane did not approve, but could not, for very shame, send me away before the visitors, especially when his wife, Mrs Blane, resplendent in green velvet, smiled so kindly and said: "Let her stay". So an atmosphere of good cheer prevailed. Last night, New Year's Eve, the guests were very merry, helped on, I fear, by the potent wine Mr Stephen produced. Some grew quite boisterous, and ran up the stairs, laughing and pushing till the little wooden animal at the top of the banister was broken off. When in the dancing Robert whispered in my ear who was to notice? Perhaps Mrs Blane . . . ? No, I do not think anyone saw as he came to me and murmured soft words of love. Surely there is not such a handsome man in the whole of England. One touch and my whole being turns to water and I melt in his arms. And in the night he told me he loved me.'

January 15th

'My happiness is all the more acute for being unexpected. When so many guests arrived and Mrs Blane asked if I would mind vacating my room and move to one of the attics I was not at all pleased to be put in among the servants. And yet it is so much better for his visits. But oh, so cold. There was a terrible blizzard here in December, luckily after the guests arrived, the snow filled the roads, burying houses, and it lies outside still in great mounds. A most terrible winter.'

February 1st

'No sign of a let up in the freezing conditions, so the guests are still here. Snow everywhere; it is said that even the railway tracks have been covered. The servants cannot get to their homes in the village, and they worry that their families may be starving. A happy time for me, for Mrs Blane has decreed that the children need not have lessons yet awhile, so I am not shut in the schoolroom. I confess I was a little shocked when I found out what some of the gentlemen do. There is gambling, and cock-fighting in the yard. I mentioned this to Robert, but he only laughed, saying, "What do you know of gentlemen?" If this had not been my own dear Robert, I would have felt he was being unkind. Perhaps I feel my position too greatly, yet I am not a mere servant. But things will surely change soon for me, for every night Robert comes to me. When will he tell his family . . . ?'

March 1st.

'The roads are passable now, so the guests have gone. Yet I have not been moved back to my old room. Robert says we have more privacy here, as indeed we do, but I am puzzled that Mrs Blane says no word. It is unthinkable that she should know—a lady in her position.

'Sometimes I think there are great mysteries in this house of a kind I do not understand.'

March 15th

'I am greatly worried. I fear I am with child. I dare not approach a physician, he would feel it his duty to inform Mrs Blane. I must tell Robert without delay, and maybe it will all be for the best. Our marriage will have to take place immediately. Why do I fear Mrs Blane? Soon I shall be sitting at table with her, as an equal, the wife of a Blane.'

March 26th

'I overheard Mrs Blane saying that Miss Sophie Travers, a simpering miss with frizzy curls, who was here at Christmas, would be an ideal wife for Robert. Greatly agitated, I managed to catch Robert as he came in today, and told him I must see him. He promised to come.'

April 1st

'What an apt date, April Fools Day! Easter next week, and outside the sun shining. Robert did not come to me so I boldly approached him in the yard and told him my fears. He hesitated, and asked me if I were mistaken. "No," I cried, "the child will be born in October. We must be married." He was thoughtful at that, and did not answer, and I was afraid. "Robert," I cried. "You told me you loved me." "Hush," he said. "Someone will hear. I must think what to do." With that I had to be content.'

Easter

'Holidays again, and guests, including Miss Sophie Travers. Robert never came to me. Nor am I again invited to dine with the family.'

April 26th

'Today the engagement was announced between Robert and Sophie Travers. I heard the news and fainted dead away. The next thing I remember was waking in my room with Mrs Blane looking at me, asking me what was the matter. And then I told her all, saying that Robert must marry me. She told me to lie and rest, and she would consult her husband.'

May 1st

'May-Day, and outside the world is rejoicing that spring is here. I can hear the birds carolling as I sit alone in my room, for I am more or less a prisoner. The guests have gone, and Mrs Blane tells me she has consulted Mr Stephen, and he has decreed that I must be confined to my room, I can no longer be allowed to mix with the children. There will be no marriage, Stephen will not allow it. Robert is to marry Miss Travers. As I have no home or family, they will not send me away, Mrs Blane said, and after the child is born they will have to consider what to do. So I weep in desolation, yet what can Robert do? Stephen is the head of the house, and Robert must obey him until he is twenty-five or he will lose his inheritance. So how could he support a wife and child without money or a home? Poor Robert.'

August

'The family are gone away on holiday which is better for me. Food is sent up from the village for me, brought by little Polly, a serving-maid, who seems to feel pity for me being alone here. I walked into the big front bedroom, where Mr Stephen and his wife rest, and saw a strange book about witchcraft which greatly disturbed me, and the name inside was Stephen Blane. Polly told me Robert was married.'

September 10th

'The family have returned, Stephen and his wife, Robert and Sophie. I am afraid, and do not know why. I asked Mrs Blane if I could see a physician, but she said that Mr Stephen said it was not necessary yet. I asked what I would do after the birth, she told me not to worry about that. Yet I do worry. I feel so desolate.'

September 20th

'Polly talks to me now when she brings my meals, and I am grateful to talk to anyone, even a serving-maid. She says there will not be another governess, the children will go away to school next month, the family will travel, Robert and his wife with them, and the house will be shut up for some months. What about me? What about my child? It will be a Blane, they must care for it. Why else would they keep me here?'

October

'I felt so ill yesterday, no pain as yet, but many strange cramps, I feel my time is approaching. I told Polly when she brought my food to tell Mrs Blane, and she slipped back to say she had done so, and that all the servants are being sent home for the weekend. I was greatly apprehensive, and asked why. "I don't know," Polly said. "Oh, Miss.

65

Can't you try to walk with us to the village? I don't like this place, funny things go on." I asked what things, and she said she heard Mr and Mrs Blane having a row, shouting about calling the gipsy. "What gipsy?" I asked, bewildered. "The witch-gipsy," she replied. "The one who cursed the Blanes." Polly is but a cottage girl, believing in superstitious nonsense, and yet . . . why am I so afraid? In the end I tried to walk to the stairs with Polly, but Mrs Blane appeared, and sent her away. Mrs Blane seemed kind, and I was ashamed of my fears.

'"Mr Stephen insisted that the servants go on holiday," she said. "But I will look after you." She has not returned as yet. Will not Stephen allow her to come? Polly had told me that Sophie is visiting her parents, but that Robert is here. What do I fear? It is so silent. I will creep down and endeavour to listen to some conversation . . . learn why the servants have been sent away . . . What mystery broods over Darrenscar?

'Tonight I will go into the yard again for a little walk—If I can, and maybe I will see Robert. Oh God, please send help to me. I am so afraid here in this attic.'

That was the end of the diary.

I closed the book and sat for a long time while the fog swirled outside. I had hoped for so much from the diary, and in the end it told me nothing. And, sad and pitiful as the tale was, I could not feel wholeheartedly sorry for the governess, though whether this denoted some lack in myself or in Mary Dean I could not say. I was shocked at the callousness of the Blanes, but I could not identify with Mary Dean.

I turned to the next item in the file of papers, a cutting from the local newspaper dated November, Eighteen eighty-three *'An inquest was held on the bodies of a woman and newly born child in the room known as the dungeon at Darrenscar. The woman was Mary Dean, aged nineteen, governess to the children of Mr Stephen Blane.'*

I read the account with interest. Mr Stephen Blane said he had been informed of the discovery of the bodies by the coachman. Yes, he knew that Dean was in a certain condition; he and his wife had sheltered the girl. Dean walked in the yard every evening for exercise, and he thought it possible that she thought she heard something in the room known as the dungeon and went to investigate, falling to her death. The woman was dead, the child nearly so, when he arrived, and he baptised the baby with the sign of the cross, which he believed to be valid in the absence of a clergyman, and would ensure Christian burial, for which he himself would be responsible. No, he had no idea who the father might be, unless it were the coachman.

'Questioned, Timothy Ridley, coachman, denied all knowledge of the woman's condition. He came

to the yard on the night in question to tend the horses, heard a cry and went to investigate. He saw the dungeon door was not fastened properly, so went down to search. When he found the woman and child he went immediately to Mr Blane.'

The coroner said that, although there was a possibility that the girl, fearing her shame, had decided to end her life, there was no positive proof of this, and a verdict of accidental death was recorded.

So the diary had not been read at the inquest. No blame was attached to the Blanes, who were to provide a decent burial. But no doubt the servants talked in the village, which was why the tragedy was still remembered today. I thought of Mary Dean, condemned in her little attic room, so afraid of mysteries. What mysteries? Why had the servants been sent away when the birth was imminent? What had Stephen Blane planned to do?

I finished the typing then turned back to the diary, reading more slowly. And then I noticed something. The pages were numbered, and *some of them were missing*. Several pages had been torn out between items written, but whereas the diary ended at page 38, both 39 and 40 were gone.

I looked at the clock. Half past twelve. Charles had, during the last weeks, taken his writing into the dining-room while I typed, but he usually called in around this time, before I finished. I had never told him of my feelings of having been here before because, since our talk about the gipsy, I felt he was too emotionally involved with it all, and I wanted to stay aloof from his involvement. Now I sat waiting for his arrival.

He came in. 'I've finished it,' I said.

'And—? What do you think?'

I sighed. 'I don't know. I don't think much of the Blanes' treatment of Mary Dean, or the way they denied knowledge at the inquest.'

'Knowledge of her death?'

'No, that it was Robert's child.'

'I told you this wasn't a make-believe story. And while I hold no brief for my ancestors, you must see it in the context of Victorian society, when prostitution was far commoner than today, and it was also common for servants to be seduced by their masters. But the masters would never talk of this before ladies, Robert would not admit to such a seduction.'

'Not even in Court?'

'He would never have been received again in society. His marriage would have been ruined.'

'It was kind of Stephen to give her a decent burial,' I said, sarcastically. 'Especially if he had taken her to the dungeon to die.'

'You think he did?'

'Well, come on,' I retorted. 'He wouldn't allow her to see a doctor, he sent the servants away. Pity for him that the coachman turned up.'

'Yes, but if he wanted to murder her, why not do it at the start? Why wait nine months?'

Why, indeed?

'What were the strange happenings she talks about?' I asked. 'The book on witchcraft she found in Stephen's room?'

He moved restlessly. 'I don't know.'

'The first Blane dabbled in witchcraft with the gipsy. Funny, I always think of witches as being bent old women with broomsticks.'

'Oh no, there have always been as many men witches as women. Young people, too. I suppose we get that impression because during the witch-hunts in the middle ages there were always old village wise women who grew herbs and so on—they were often put to death as well.'

'So,' I said. 'There may have been some reason for keeping Mary Dean there—and her newborn child . . .' And immediately I was filled with horror and didn't know why. Horror of some un-nameable thing that I could not bear.

Charles said: 'We don't know—'

'Of course we don't know the whole truth, because some of the pages are missing. Did you notice?'

'Yes.'

'Do you know where they are?'

'Destroyed, I should imagine.'

70

'When did you first read the diary, Charles?'

'About five years ago. They were missing then.'

'Is there any possibility that they are still around? Has anyone looked?'

He frowned. 'Not to my knowledge.'

I was silent. I resolved to search for those papers. It seemed a hopeless task, but maybe they would throw some light on the strange happenings Mary Dean feared, the funny goings-on Polly spoke of. Mary Dean had ended by saying she was going to listen to the Blanes' conversation—what had she heard?

I shivered. I must find the missing pages—if they existed, and would say as little to Charles as possible.

I was thoughtful as I went into the kitchen and took the big tray that was to carry my lunch and Richard's. For the time being I left Richard with Aunt Kitty in the mornings, while I worked on the typing. As soon as this was finished I intended to tackle Charles about bringing him down, for I was determined not to sit upstairs all winter like Mary Dean.

I went into Richard's room. He was walking round the bed, I had insisted on this, and I smiled to see him. Aunt Kitty put down her interminable knitting and stood up.

'Come girl, you are late,' she said.

There had been several occasions when Aunt Kitty had 'gone into the past' as I termed it, but

71

never, since that first time, had I let it annoy me so much. Now, when she addressed me as one of the lower orders I just laughed it off.

But this time was different. This time I felt a trembling fear of the mistress of the house, a fear such as Mary Dean must have known. Then she was gone, and I sat on the bed, shivering and afraid.

★　　★　　★

The fog still hung around after lunch, and I wondered whether I should take Richard for his usual walk. He was a healthy child, but fog was not good for anyone.

I wanted to go out, inside, a cocoon of fear was beginning to wrap around me as the fog wrapped the moors. So I ran up to Richard's room, where Aunt Kitty sat still with her knitting. 'You're not going out?' she asked, as I picked up Richard's clothes.

'Just for a short time,' I said.

Down again, I put a woollen hood on Richard's head, enveloped him in a long scarf, and put on his little wellingtons. 'You look like Father Christmas,' I told him.

I was tremendously pleased with Richard's progress. In a few short weeks he had changed from a silent, sullen child to an eager boy, not very talkative, he would never be that, but happy. And learning to walk well.

We went outside, and I held his hand tight, while the fog pressed clammy fingers on us. When he said: 'Let me go, Dee,' I loosed his hand. 'It's a nasty day,' I said. 'But we'll go into the warm kitchen soon, and have a nice drink with Mrs Appleby.'

He toddled along, clasping the wall, and I followed, thinking of Alan. This, too, was something that had been left in abeyance. Three times I had seen him in York, in the evenings, and I had gone alone, merely asking Charles' permission to take the Mini, which was always granted. So Alan and I dined and danced, and in the car he kissed me passionately. That was all, three casual meetings, as any girl and boy would have. So why the secrecy?

I saw Richard fall, heard him cry: 'Dee, what's that?' and I ran forward, cursing myself for dreaming about Alan. Then I grabbed Richard and pulled him back from the open door of the dungeon.

I stood, shaking. The wooden door leading down to the dungeon was always fastened. Now it was wide open and yes, held back by a catch on the wall. The gap yawned before me, and again I felt the fear. I made to close the door then paused. Didn't they say Jim Bradshaw used it as a cellar, for storage? Was he perhaps, down there? I remembered that Alan had said a torch was always kept there, and I found it, hanging near the opening. So there could not be anyone down, or they'd have taken the torch. To be sure, I shone it down the steps and called.

My voice echoed faintly, but no one replied. The torch shone on the damp steps, but did not reach the bottom. Shuddering, I closed and fastened the door, leaning my back on it, gasping.

Richard watched me with puzzled eyes.

I bent down and held him in my arms. 'You must never, never go through that door. Do you understand?'

'Yes.' His eyes stared into mine, unafraid.

'It's dangerous,' I said. 'The door must be kept shut.'

I took his hand and led him away. But the afternoon was spoilt. We'd go back indoors.

The kitchen was warm and bright as always, and Mrs Appleby was preparing tea. 'I'm glad you came in,' she said. 'I've prepared a casserole for dinner, perhaps you could put it in the oven later.'

'Of course. Are you going now?'

'I must. My married daughter, in Charby, the next village, is pregnant, doctor's ordered her to rest. I'll have to go over to help out. But I'll try to come once a week.'

'I'm sorry,' I said, concerned. And then. 'I'll miss you.'

'You'll be all right,' Mrs Appleby said. 'Don't let 'em get you down, funny old lot they are.'

I smiled, and she fastened her coat and left.

I surveyed the scene outside. It looked as though Richard's little outings were over for this year. But he must keep on exercising, and if I had to do the cooking, either I had him down here with me, or left him to Aunt Kitty. And I knew which it would be. I would speak to Charles today.

I took a cup of tea into the study, but he was busy writing, so I said nothing. I could wait. Back in the kitchen I heard the outside door open and wondered if it were Mrs Appleby again. But it was Alan.

'Dee,' he cried. 'And all alone.' He put his arms round me and kissed me soundly.

'Are you home for the day?' I asked, when I could speak.

'Yes. Not much doing there. Dee, darling Dee, why don't we slip out for an hour? Take the boy upstairs.'

'In the fog?' I asked.

'Oh, we needn't go far. Just to a little pub I know.'

I would have loved to go, but I shook my head. 'No, Alan, I can't.'

He was still holding me. 'What do you mean, you can't?' He was kissing my cheek, my neck.

'It's my job to look after Richard,' I said.

'But you can take him to his room.'

'I think it's wrong to push him away

upstairs,' I said. 'He should stay here with the family. Why should he be kept out of sight all the time?'

'Well,' Alan moved uncomfortably. 'You know how Charles feels about it.'

'But why, Alan? Richard is his child. If his mother didn't want him, surely his father should be even more fond of him.'

Alan moved to the window, moodily, but I was persistent. 'Why did his mother leave him anyway? What sort of mother was she? Tell me about it, Alan.'

'Oh. There was a big row, and she left, that's all.'

'That's all? How old was Richard then?'

'Oh, quite small.'

'How could she? But I suppose it was Charles, wasn't it? He forced her to go.'

'In a way.'

'It's monstrous,' I said. 'Why did he—?'

'Leave it now, Dee,' Alan said. 'It's over. Come on, just for an hour. No one will know.'

If only he hadn't said that. 'No,' I replied. 'And not only because of Richard.'

'What then?'

'This business of slipping out on the quiet. Why should we? Why should I be treated like a—a little governess?'

He smiled, that smile I loved so well, his good humour restored. 'Well, I declare,' he mimicked in a shrill falsetto. 'You've been reading that old diary.'

'Yes, I have. And I don't care much for the way the Blanes conduct their affairs.'

Now his voice changed to a deep baritone, and he twirled imaginary moustaches. 'Tonight I will make you mine—or you'll be turned out into the snow.'

I laughed in spite of myself. 'Stop it, Alan, you are a fool.'

'So are you, talking about those old events. What on earth has that to do with us?'

Quite a lot, according to Charles. But Alan wasn't Charles, and trying to pin him down to a serious conversation was like trying to catch the wind. I asked 'What do you think of Mary Dean?'

His answer surprised me. 'I agree she was treated badly. But I've read the diary, and Mary Dean did not once say she loved Robert. She wanted to marry him to become someone important. She didn't love him.'

I realised that Alan, with unerring accuracy, had put his finger on the one thing I had found lacking in the diary. Mary Dean had never said she loved Robert. Nor had she thought much about the child to be born, though that was perhaps natural in the circumstances. I said. 'Well, Robert didn't love her.'

'So they deserved each other, wouldn't you say?'

'She didn't deserve to be murdered.'

'*If* she was murdered. There's no proof of that. But enough of them. How about coming out?'

'No, Alan, I meant what I said. If your mother objects to me—'

'It isn't just you, Dee, it's all girls.'

'She wants you to remain a bachelor all your life?'

I hadn't wanted to get on the subject of marriage. And yet, the thought crossed my mind fleetingly. If we were married, the gipsy's curse would no longer apply to me. I wouldn't be a light o' love, I'd be a wife.

'I think,' Alan was saying, 'my mother, in her little dream world, has a fantasy that I'll meet some noble heroine with pots of money.'

'You think of nothing but money,' I said, crossly.

'Don't we all? We're just honest about it.'

I wondered if he were subtly warning me that marriage was out for us.

'Charles doesn't seem to approve of our meeting either,' I said. 'What's it to him what you do? You should put your foot down, Alan.'

'You know I don't want to upset him just now. Not until he's agreed to sell the land. That would help us all, Mother, too.'

'How?' I asked, practically. 'If the money goes to him?'

'Because I should get a hefty commission on the sale.'

'You work for a property company then. I see.' That was why Alan had his job, in order to persuade Charles to sell. Well, I supposed that's how things were done. 'Does your mother know about it?' I asked.

'About my job? No.'

'Why not? Why all this secrecy in everything here?'

'Because she wouldn't understand. And she might let it slip to Charles.'

'I don't think she would,' I said. 'I think you underestimate your mother.'

There was a pause. 'You're not coming then?' Alan asked.

'No.'

'In that case, I'll go alone.' And he went to the door.

We've quarrelled, I thought, drearily. And yet I could not think I was wrong.

I turned back to Richard, who had been sitting on the rug, looking through one of his picture-books. 'Pussy-cat,' he said.

'Pussy-cat it is,' I said, delighted. I put the casserole in the oven and sat down to read to him until Charles came in.

He was late, and I thought he looked tired, but I made no move to take Richard away. 'Mrs. Appleby's gone,' I said, casually. 'And won't be coming every day now.'

'No,' he said, sighing. 'I was going to ask you—'

'If I'll do the cooking,' I finished.

'Could you cope? The typing is finished now.'

'I can cope,' I said. 'But what about Richard? If I can't spend my time with him in his room, then he must stay down here with me.'

There was a pause which seemed to go on and on, while outside the fog pressed relentlessly on the window panes.

'I think it's best for him,' I went on, breathless now. 'He must be treated as a normal member of the family.'

'And if I object?'

'But why in heaven's name should you object?' I was getting angry now, and wished after all I'd taken Richard upstairs before I spoke, I'd criticized Aunt Kitty for just this same thing. 'Wait a minute,' I said. 'Don't go away, we must have this out.'

I picked Richard up, carried him to his room. 'Stay just for a minute, darling,' I said. 'I'll bring your milk up and get you into bed. Won't be long.'

When I returned to the kitchen Charles was standing looking out into the fog. I said to his back: 'I've had to leave him alone. You must see it isn't right.'

He did not reply.

'When I came here that child was absolutely neglected,' I shouted. 'I know Aunt Kitty means well, but she just kept him in bed all day, and it's wrong. Do you know that he didn't have a single toy of his own? Why do you treat him so? Is it because you think him handicapped? That's what your advertisement said. He isn't handicapped at all, just late in walking. Some children are late talking, it doesn't mean anything. But now he's growing into a lovely little boy, yet you can't bear to look at him. Why?'

'It's nothing to do with his walking,' Charles said at last.

'Is it because your wife left you? But why take it out on the child for what his mother did? Obviously she was wrong, or was she? Did you treat her badly?'

He said, his lips white, 'It wasn't quite like that.'

'Then what was it like? Oh, I know it isn't my business, and frankly I couldn't care less, except for Richard.'

'There was another man,' he said.

I was a little taken aback. 'So that explains something at least.'

'What does it explain?'

'Why you were so upset. She was so beautiful you loved her hopelessly, you found out she had another man . . .'

'You little fool,' he said and his voice was cutting. 'Don't you understand what I'm trying to say? Richard isn't my child at all.'

CHAPTER FOUR

The silence was acute. It pressed in on us, and I wished something would break the stillness, if only the cry of a bird. I wanted to say I was sorry, but knowing how Charles had reacted to my sympathy once before I said nothing. He must make the first move.

'You are right, she was beautiful,' he said at last. 'Though that means nothing without charm, personality. She had a lovely face. I even, God help me, found myself quoting poetry: *She walks in beauty like the night—*'

He was facing me now, but he didn't see me. 'I'd never believed in love,' he said. 'I wasn't the marrying type. Alan might run after every skirt,'—I winced—'but not me. Oh well, the bigger they are the harder they fall.' He gave a mirthless laugh.

Lucky Marianne, I thought, to have such love. 'But what went wrong?' I whispered.

'Who knows? My love wasn't enough?'

'You told me once you were too busy to see much of her.'

'I was. Busy writing, working the farm, trying to support everybody. Alan and his debts, Aunt Kitty, Marianne herself. What else could I do?'

'I'm sorry,' I said. 'I must say that whether

you like it or not.'

'It doesn't matter. I don't want to be an object of pity, but on the other hand it's only fair to tell you the truth.'

'This does seem an unhappy house, doesn't it?' I said. 'No one is happy for long. I noticed that in the history. So many die young—'

'Yes, but again, you must take it in the context of the age. People didn't live so long in the old days.'

'Were your parents happily married?' I ventured.

'As far as I know. My father was killed when I was two, my mother when I was four.'

'Alan's father?'

'When he was three. I was eleven, just starting grammar school.'

'So—Aunt Kitty has been managing things since then till you took over?'

'I took over from the age of eleven,' he corrected. 'I came home from school to do the accounts, helped with the farm. Even when I had that newspaper job I found it difficult—that's why I wanted to work at home.'

'You've had it rough,' I said.

'I thought I'd find a little happiness with Marianne. But I should have known I wouldn't, not here.'

'Do you like Darrenscar?' I asked.

'Like it? I've never thought about it. It's my

home.'

'Yes. But the way you have to work to keep it going, it does seem that you're trapped here—' I broke off.

'What else would I do?' he asked, bleakly, and I felt pity for him then, realising he was trapped inside himself.

'I'm glad you told me,' I said. 'And I still say that Richard is not to blame. I think—' now I picked my words carefully. 'Grief such as yours can be selfish, you are shutting everyone out. Grown ups can fend for themselves, but not a child.'

I expected he'd fly into a rage, but he did not, he stared thoughtfully ahead. 'Grief selfish?' he asked. 'I never thought of it in that way. But you can't expect me to love him can you? Every time I see him it reminds me of her—and him, the man. Can't you understand?'

'Yes. But you could try to be kind. Because if he's not allowed to live a normal life then he would be better in a home, as you said at first.'

That shook him as I intended.

'All right,' he said at last. 'You win, Dee. Bring him downstairs, and I'll at least try to be civil. But don't expect too much. And this is on condition that you stay.'

'Blackmail,' I said, but my heart was light. I ran back to Richard, sitting alone in his bedroom, and swept him into my arms. 'We're going to have a lovely time from now on,' I said, and hoped it was true.

★   ★   ★

That night at dinner I brought up the subject of
the dungeon, and the open door. 'It's
dangerous,' I said. 'Richard could have got
down there.'

'I shouldn't think so, if you were with him,'
Charles said mildly. 'I expect it was Jim,
though I haven't seen him around.'

'The door should be kept closed,' I said
firmly.

They all looked surprised, and Alan said:
'You do have a thing about that old dungeon,
don't you?'

He was right, and I knew I could never
explain to them the terror I felt when I saw it.
Whatever evil the house held was somehow
concentrated in the dungeon.

Charles said: 'All right, I'll see that the door
is kept closed. Alan, have a word with Jim
Bradshaw, will you?'

Alan nodded, and I sighed with relief.

'Do you realise?' Aunt Kitty said. 'It will
soon be Christmas?'

'Will you be going home, Dee?' Charles
asked me.

'I don't know.' I hesitated. Since I'd been
here I'd heard nothing from Aunt Meg,
although I wrote to her when I arrived. 'I doubt

it,' I ended.

'If only we could have a party,' Aunt Kitty said.

'I think we should have a party for Richard,' I said. 'Get a tree, and toys.'

'You mean, ask other *children*?' Charles couldn't have sounded more astonished if I'd wanted to fill the house with hobgoblins.

'Not necessarily,' I replied. 'I don't suppose we know any other children, do we? Just among ourselves.'

'You mean pulling crackers and giving each other presents—here?' Alan asked. 'The thought slays me.'

'Is it so funny?' I said, coldly.

'Funny? It's hilarious.'

'Then,' I said, 'Aunt Kitty and I will have a party.'

Aunt Kitty clapped her hands like a child. 'Lovely. And we'll wear fancy dress.'

Why not? I thought, recklessly. If it makes her happy.

Dinner over, Charles and Aunt Kitty went to bed. Not, I realised, because they believed in early hours at Darrenscar so much as to get away from each other. I sighed as I removed the plates.

I washed up. There were no curtains at the kitchen window, and for the first time I wished there were. The fog outside was unnerving. I felt disorientated.

I heard a sound behind me and started. Then a soft voice said: 'Dee.'

'Alan.'

'We haven't quarrelled, have we? I couldn't bear it if we had.'

He came up to me and slid his arm around my waist. I smiled. 'No, we haven't quarrelled.'

He kissed me then, and all the feeling I tried to forget came back in full force. 'I love you,' he whispered. 'You know I do.'

I clung to him, kissing him back. The fog didn't matter now. Nor Charles. Nor Aunt Kitty. Nothing mattered but Alan. His arms were tight around me, I drowned in his kisses. He whispered. 'Let me come to your room.'

Why not? I thought. That way I'd make him mine forever.

He came to my room last night. I'd heard those words before. In the diary. Mary Dean's diary. I moved away.

'Please, Dee.' Still he held me.

'No.'

'Why not? We love each other.'

'I'm sorry, Alan.'

He didn't say any more. And as he went upstairs I knew I was afraid. The powers in Darrenscar didn't allow happiness.

★   ★   ★

In the morning, when I woke, the fog was still

heavy. I remembered that Mrs Appleby wouldn't be coming, that I'd have to get breakfast. I went down, and found the postman had already been, fog or no fog. There was a letter for me from Aunt Meg. I read it, quickly at first, then again, more slowly.

Aunt Meg was giving up her house, because she could not afford to keep it going alone. She was going to live with a friend, a widow. So she would not be able to ask me there again, there would not be room . . .

I put the letter down with mixed feelings. First, the antagonism Aunt Meg always aroused in me swept through me, and then remorse. I had thought her so grudging towards me, and yet it seemed she had been quite poor. I thought of my talk with Charles yesterday, when I had been giving out good advice, talking about selfishness. Was I any better? Was I so different from Mary Dean?

But one thing was certain. Now I was alone.

I cooked the breakfast in silence, brought Richard downstairs, and braced myself to tell Aunt Kitty that I intended looking after him in future. The opportunity arose when Charles and Alan had gone out of the kitchen.

'I'll look after Richard while you clean,' Aunt Kitty said.

'No need, Aunt Kitty, thanks,' I replied. 'Richard is staying down here with me.'

'But Charles—'

'Charles agrees,' I said.

'I'm perfectly capable of looking after him.' A hurt tone had crept into her voice, and I felt guilty.

'I know, Aunt Kitty, but he is getting a handful now he begins to walk. I think it's better this way.'

'Oh, well.' She turned away. 'I'll feed my chickens.'

She did not offer to help with the housework, so I hardened my heart again.

Eleven o'clock and I sat Richard on the sofa, made coffee, and took a steaming mug into Charles.

He was not working, he was sitting staring down at his history of Darrenscar, and I felt a momentary pity as I stared at his stern, unbending face. 'Still brooding, Charles?' I asked.

'Thanks, Dee. Yes, I suppose I am.'

'You never go out,' I said. 'Not to—to enjoy yourself, I mean. Maybe you should. Let everything go—' my voice trailed away at his look.

'It wouldn't make any difference,' he said.

'But you seem so unhappy here,' I argued, boldly.

'I haven't told you everything . . .' he said 'And—I can't . . . even now, can't discuss it.' He gave me a brief glance and his eyes were tortured. 'You shouldn't have come here, Dee.

Maybe you should go away . . .'

I didn't stay to argue with him, but went back to the kitchen, and even this usually bright room seemed dull today, closed in by fog. For once I did not go straight to Richard, but went to the window and looked out. Nothingness. The fog covered everything, closed in on me, trapped me. I held the sill for I was trembling.

There was evil in this house. Charles knew it and I knew it. Maybe all old houses with violent histories hold within themselves some taint of the turbulence that occurred. But if the evil manifested itself again how could I or anyone conquer it? Exorcism? None of the Blanes went to a church, no clergyman called at Darrenscar.

I turned from the window. Richard sat on the sofa, looking at me, his dark eyes enormous in his white face. He did not speak or smile, but his face seemed to be pleading.

I couldn't go, couldn't leave him. I was trapped by my very love. I ran to him and took him in my arms.

*　　　*　　　*

The fogs disappeared, but mists still hung over the moors, sometimes swirling along in patches, like falling clouds, sometimes hanging low. Then came gales, when the whole house seemed to shudder, the tall trees outside bent in supplication, as the wind howled round the house like a soul in torment. The cold began to bite, there were sharp frosts at night, and I would wake to find my windows covered with delicate tracery, and outside a spider's web hung, an intricate pattern in white lace.

I took Richard to York again, and this time I did not tell Alan I was going. Partly because it was dark before four o'clock, and I wanted to get back as soon as I could. Partly because I felt, when thinking of our so-called affair, so helpless. Meeting in secret would lead only to one thing, I knew, and I would be powerless to prevent it. I was afraid of my feelings. Better we kept apart, for the present.

The doctor was pleased with Richard's progress, saying he was much livelier in every way, and in a year he should have caught up, be quite normal.

'You will be staying with him, I trust,' said the doctor, and I nodded, smiling, 'I hope so.'

I took Richard to the shops, to see Santa Claus, and this made him happy. On the way home he even began to sing, a little tuneless ditty that brought tears to my eyes. Darrenscar came in sight, and I received the same sense of dread I always did. So, I thought, must escaped prisoners feel when they were caught and sent back. I must get out more, I told myself. I could use the car, I would take Richard into the village. Now the fogs had gone there would be no problem.

So next day I drove down the hill to where the village sat squatly in the valley, and entered the little store, where plump Mrs Briggs presided behind the counter, and several women waited to be served.

'You're from Darrenscar,' one of the women said to me. 'How do you like it?'

'All right,' I answered.

She sniffed. 'Nobody round here 'ull work for the Blanes. Only Mrs Appleby, and she's a foreigner.'

'A foreigner?' I was startled.

'Aye, she's not from these parts. She married Ted Appleby.

'I see,' I said, suddenly conscious of my southern accent.

'Aye, there's a lot of bitterness against the Blanes,' Mrs Briggs said, folding her arms.

'I suppose,' I remarked, 'you remember about Mary Dean, who was found dead.'

'I don't remember it happening, of course,' the first woman spoke again. 'But my dad talked about it. Got it from his dad.'

I was excited. 'And what did he say?'

'Why, that she was murdered, what else? Polly Briginshaw saw her alive and well in the morning. Next thing she was found in that dungeon, dead. And all the servants sent away.'

'My grandad found her,' said the other woman, unexpectedly.

'He was the coachman?' I was more excited than ever.

'Aye. He were only a young man, and they tried to put the blame on him.'

'How did he find her?'

'Went up that night to see to the horses, an' heard a baby cry. He was outside in the yard, and couldn't tell where the sound came from. He looked in the stables, and then went down the dungeon.'

'I don't see how he could hear anything from up top, Mrs Patterson,' said Mrs Briggs.

'Well, he did. An' he went down and found the woman lying there, and the baby just born. The woman were dead. He was shocked, my grandad.'

I shivered.

'An' he found some papers with her,' said Mrs Patterson.

I pricked up my ears. 'Papers? What papers?'

'I dunno, they took 'em away, the Blanes. It were as if she'd been writing summat, that poor dead soul.'

'How could she, in the dark?' asked Mrs Briggs, sceptically.

'I dunno, but that's what he said. An' he tried to tell 'em at the inquest, but nobody would listen to him, they blamed him.'

Obviously the feeling against the Blanes ran high in the village, with some justification, I thought. But what papers were with Mary

Dean? Had she taken her diary with her to the dungeon? Hardly, one would have thought. But if it had been in her pocket or reticule or whatever Victorian governesses carried as a handbag, and it probably would be—she'd hardly want to leave it lying around—then yes, she'd have it there. But if she had been taken to her death in the dungeon she would hardly feel like writing a diary, especially in the middle of childbirth. Unless . . .

If she had written anything, then it could only be one thing. The name of her murderer.

I left the shop and took Richard back to the car. I wanted to get back to search the house.

★   ★   ★

Yet it was several days before I was able to search. I was pretty busy in the daytime, the evenings were taken up with preparing dinner, and after that, washing up. And although Charles had more or less given his permission, I knew Alan would just laugh if he saw me, while Aunt Kitty would probably say I was usurping my position or something of the sort. In the end I decided to wait until everyone was in bed.

I wondered where to start. If the Blanes had taken the papers surely they would be in the big front bedroom. As soon as the house had settled into slumber I crept along and opened the door.

I switched on the light. There was an

incredible amount of furniture in this room, as though all the old stuff had been brought in here for storage. It would take days to go through all this. But in the corner was a small oak bureau, and I made my way to this.

None of the drawers was locked, and most of them contained papers. I sat down and ran through them. There was nothing referring to Mary Dean.

I put them back with a sigh, and drew out a small black volume. 'A Study in Witchcraft and the Black Arts.'

I drew it out, opened to the title page. *Stephen Blane* was written in bold, black handwriting.

This was the book Mary Dean had written about. Had she read it? And why hadn't Charles mentioned that it was around?

I closed the drawer, and took the book back to my room. I was just about to get into bed when I had another thought. I was in Mary Dean's room—but when she was expecting the child, no, even before that, when the guests arrived, she had been moved into an attic. I had never seen the attics and had a sudden inexplicable desire to explore them. So I crept from my room again.

The back stairs were next to my room, and at the end of the passage. They led down to the yard, and up to the attics, the servants' bedrooms. Quietly, I went up. It was dark here, and when I pressed a switch no light came on. Obviously no one bothered with these attics now.

I could faintly see a corridor, and a number of rooms leading off. To the right was a small alcove with another door. Surely, I thought, this must have been for Mary Dean. This would have been ideal for Robert to visit her in the night; it was, in a way, quite private. I opened the door.

Again no light, but a ragged moon shone fitfully into the tiny room. I could see a brass bedstead and mattress, a wash-hand stand with jug and bowl, a chest of drawers. And I knew this had been the room, for as I looked round the old familiarity came to me.

I sat on the bed and a strange thing happened, and to this day I cannot tell if it was a dream . . . at the time I felt it was happening to me.

Mary Dean was lying on the bed, and she was in pain. And she said: 'My time is come. Oh, my poor baby. I have thought so little of you, and now it is too late. I shall never be able to love you. If only I could have my time over again, to love you as you should be loved. Now it is too late. If only I'd known . . . Now you will have to lose, my little Richard . . . Oh, for my time over again . . .'

And in the dream I was Mary Dean, and I was writing, but as in a nightmare, could not see what I wrote. I stepped out of bed and knelt on the floor. There was a loose floorboard, and I prised it up, put the paper underneath, then lay on the bed again.

I came to the present, bathed in sweat. I was lying on the bed, the moon shining clearly now, lighting up the narrow room, the brass bedsteads. Somewhere a clock struck twelve. It was very cold.

Had I been dreaming? I had looked at my watch as I came up the stairs, it had been ten minutes to twelve. I knew this was no dream.

My teeth chattered. I thought of Mary Dean writing . . . hiding the paper . . . could it have been true? There was one way to find out, to prove once and for all if I had imagined everything, or if—

Shivering, I stood up. It was so cold, and the moonlight did not give sufficient light to see under the bed. I had no torch, no candle even, though there were plenty in the kitchen. But that was a long way away, better I fetched the electric bulb from my room . . .

I crept silently down the stairs, left my door open and took the bulb from the bedside lamp. Up again, and I stood on the bed to fit the bulb. It fitted, and the light came on.

I moved to the end of the bed. Yes, one board was loose, and I prised it up, breaking off one end as I did so. And I stared in disappointment. There were several wires underneath, evidently the electricians had worked here. That would account for the loose board. There was no paper.

But the board was long, perhaps the other end? I tried again. Here, resting on a wooden slat, embedded in dust, was a paper, preserved in the darkness.

With trembling fingers I opened it, and began to read.

'*I must write everything so that people will know the truth, but am so shocked with horror I cannot yet bear to put down the words. I know now what they plan to do. I am so shocked I can hardly breathe. If only I had guessed . . . Now it is too late to get away, now the pains are upon me and the servants sent away. Is it too late? What can I do to save my child from such treachery, such wickedness, such baseness, such evil? I hear steps, I will finish later—in full—*'

That was all.

Carefully I replaced the board, took out the light bulb, and with the paper in my hand crept downstairs. I put the paper in my bag, then undressed and slipped between the sheets. I was so cold I felt I'd never be warm again.

I was beginning, just beginning, to unravel the mystery. But would the evil which Mary Dean mentioned let me continue?

Fear overwhelmed me, and it was a long time before I slept.

I woke late the next morning, and I think I was still in a state of shock. I burned the bacon, and couldn't eat anything myself, so that both Charles and Alan asked me if I weren't well.

'I'm all right,' I said, colourlessly. 'I couldn't sleep last night.'

'Leave the work today,' Charles said. 'We'll open a tin of something for lunch.'

But I wanted to work. I didn't want to sit and think.

It was Saturday, Alan was at home, but after breakfast he returned to his room. Charles, as always, went into the study. I wanted to tell him about the paper, but this would mean explaining the whole business and I didn't feel up to it at the moment. I felt a strange horror of what had happened to me, there was no enjoyment in the knowledge I had, only fear. I read somewhere that people who have 'second sight', do not welcome, but fear it. I understood.

I fetched Richard down and went to wash up. Aunt Kitty made things worse by fussing around. I was glad when she went to prepare the chickens' food. 'Now it's cold,' she said, 'they can't go into the field. We keep them in the stable.'

'I don't know why you bother,' I said.

'I don't want to, really,' Aunt Kitty confided.

'But I have to; there have always been chickens at Darrenscar.'

I grunted, and walked to the window as she trotted out with food. She went to the stable, then scattered grain over the yard, and the chickens came out, several black cockerels, and a number of assorted hens. I thought of Mary Dean, and the cock-fighting. At least, that didn't go on today, or did it? I wouldn't have been surprised.

I followed Charles' instructions and opened tins for lunch, even managed to eat a little myself. I hoped Mrs Appleby would soon be back.

Alas for my hopes. She rang in the afternoon. Her daughter had nearly lost the baby, and she had to stay in bed for the present. Mrs Appleby was sorry, but it looked as though she'd be unable to get back for some time.

The sky was clear today, though there was no sun, and there had been a sharp frost in the night. Alan came into the kitchen wearing his overcoat, and when I turned back to the window, sat down.

'You know, Dee, I've been thinking. About us.'

'Oh?'

'Turn round, Dee, let me see you. That's better. Now, I know you think I am playing, but I'm not. I do love you.'

'Do you, Alan?' Even to me my voice

sounded lack-lustre.

'But what can I do? If in three years' time I get my money I can start my own little business.'

'Doing what?' I asked, practically.

'Something in property. I am learning now.'

'Learning what?' I asked. 'Buying and selling?'

'Yes. And at the moment I just get commission. But if I left the house now I'd never be able to come back again, would lose my inheritance, would even lose any hope of inheriting Darrenscar should anything happen to Charles.'

'And all that lovely land for building,' I said.

'Don't sound so disapproving, Dee.'

'Sorry,' I said. 'But aren't you forgetting Richard?'

'Richard?'

'Oh, I know that—that it's rumoured he's not Charles' child. And I'm not an expert in law. But surely he is legally Charles' son, unless someone proves otherwise.'

'And no one would do that,' Alan said, bitterly. 'In fact I imagine Charles would claim Richard as his own just to keep me out.'

I shook my head sadly. 'Such bitterness between you. Oh, Alan, wouldn't you be happier away, let it all go?'

'I can't, Dee. There's mother to think of. She hasn't known any other life since she married.

Her parents refused to see her again, as you know.'

'Yes.' Fleetingly I wondered why. Was there any other reason for the break, did they know something . . . ?

'Don't you see how hard it's been for her?' Alan was asking. 'I have to make it up somehow.'

'I don't really see why,' I said slowly. 'But I suppose you've been brought up to think so, haven't you?' He had been smothered by his mother, just as Richard would have been if I had not interfered. Now he was unable to make his own decisions, and I had to face the fact.

'Do you want to marry me?' I asked, bluntly.

'That's what I was saying. And in three years' time—'

'In three years' time we can move away,' I said.

'It might not be necessary to move. I could live here as I do now.'

'All of us?' I asked. 'You and Charles and Aunt Kitty?'

'And Richard.'

'Yes.' He had this uncanny knack of hitting nails on the head, as if sometimes he could read my thoughts. If I married him and moved away what about Richard?

'You're so different from anyone I've ever known,' he was saying. 'It's as though we belong together, isn't it?'

'Yes,' I said. 'When you were a tadpole and I was a fish, I loved you even then.'

'What?'

'I don't think I've got it right,' I said. 'But it explains what I mean.'

'I know something better than that,' Charles said, walking in:

> '"Strangers drawn from the ends of the earth, jewelled and plumed were we,
> "She was Queen of the Inca race and I was King of the Sea.
> "Under the stars beyond our stars where the new forged meteors glow,
> "Hotly we stormed Valhalla, a million years ago."'

I turned in amazement. 'Charles!' I exclaimed.

'Kipling,' said Charles. 'And it ends:

> '"They will come back, come back again, as long as the red earth rolls.
> "He never squandered a leaf or a tree, do you think He would squander souls?"'

Alan muttered something and went out. Charles returned to the study. I was alone with my thoughts.

★   ★   ★

On Monday the fog came down again. It was not a dirty yellow fog, as in London, but white, ghost-like. The kitchen was an oasis of light in a formless world. Alan came in and sat down.

'I'm not going to work today,' he announced.

'Why not?' That was Charles.

'Because of the fog.'

'That's never stopped you when you wanted to go out.'

'Well, it won't hurt to take a day off.'

'Why don't you go to the farm for once?' Charles asked.

'What? Look around the moors for a few sheep lost in the fog? You must be joking.'

'There are other things you could do.'

'Why,' Alan asked, angrily, 'are you always playing the heavy big brother, or cousin? You always did, all my life. I was extravagant, careless, the black sheep. I wouldn't work. And you think you're so much better? What sort of life is it that you lead? You're like a mole, working away, never coming up to see the sun, you neglect everything and everyone who gets in your way—'

'Alan!' Charles was so angry it was almost a shout. I was afraid something would happen. I cried, in a voice that bordered on the hysterical:

'Stop it! Stop it! This eternal bickering gets me down. Can't you see how miserable you make other people?'

Charles drew a breath. 'I'm sorry, Dee. You told us once before how ill-mannered we were. You're right.'

Alan muttered something, and flung himself out of the house.

'I'm sorry,' I said again. 'But things seem to be getting on my nerves a bit.'

'I'm not surprised,' said Charles. He paced up and down, thinking. Then: 'Is it true?' he asked.

'Is what true?'

'Alan's description of me.'

'We-ell.' I swept a duster aimlessly around the table. 'I suppose it is, in a way.'

He didn't answer, and I hurried on. 'Oh, I understand. You've had to work hard all these years, as you told me. But if you were always putting Alan down I can understand his point of view, too. Alan has good points, Charles.'

'Such as?'

'He's lovable, and kind.'

'And I'm not?'

I said: 'There seems such enmity between you. It must have started years ago, when Alan was quite young.'

'And I called him a mother's boy and mocked him. Oh yes, I did. Some day he was bound to get his revenge.'

'Oh, Charles!'

'Don't worry, Dee. I'm going back to the study now, back to my mole-like activities. You see, the trouble is, someone has to work. If we'd left things to Alan, we'd have gone hand in hand to the workhouse. Dammit,' he suddenly shouted, 'we have so little capital left, I'm working for Alan now, for the money he will get.'

'You could sell the land,' I said.

'Dee, I've explained about that.'

'I know. And it's nothing to do with me. But your reason for not selling is purely selfish. It's not because you want to preserve rural areas or anything of that sort, it's just because you don't want to see people. And so you are forced to work harder. Yes, I can see Alan's point.'

'You think I'm punishing myself?'

'Oh, lord, I don't know. I just know that some people are like that, Aunt Meg was. She had to work, and I do feel sorry for her now. But when I lived with her I never did, and for the same reason. She worked hard, and because she did, she thought everyone else should, too. She was very self-righteous about it.'

'Really.' He gave a half-laugh that sounded piqued. 'I'm getting a true insight into my character this morning.'

'I'm sorry,' I said. 'But you did ask me. Now you can tell me my faults if you like.'

'Not now, I haven't time. I'll write a memo.'

I smiled faintly as he left the kitchen.

★　　★　　★

Alan came back for lunch, but the atmosphere was strained, even Aunt Kitty had little to say. I washed up, hoping that Alan would stay with me, but he didn't, he went up to his room, as did Aunt Kitty. Charles, as always, returned to the study.

I looked outside. The fog had lifted a little, it was possible to see the yard, so I decided to take Richard for his little walk. I put on his hat and coat, wrapped a scarf around his neck, when Charles came in.

'Going out?' he asked.

'Just into the yard.'

'I have to go upstairs. There's a paper somewhere in my room though heaven knows where. I must search for it. Will you listen for the phone while I'm away?'

'Of course,' I said. 'I'll hear it outside.'

I took Richard's hand, and he walked unsteadily along, holding the wall. The fog was not too thick here, though it was impossible to see farther than a few yards. We'd not been away five minutes when the phone rang.

'Richard, we have to go in,' I said. 'We'll come out again.'

'Oh, no, Dee-Dee. Stay out.'

'You're getting naughty,' I told him. 'Well, I suppose that's a good sign.' The phone rang insistently. I had to go, or Charles would be angry, and I'd upset him enough for one day. I

107

looked along the yard. Nothing in sight, Richard would be all right for a few moments. I ran indoors and picked up the phone.

'Hallo.' It was a girl's voice. 'I'd like to speak to Mr Charles Blane.'

'Just a moment.' I ran to the stairs. 'Charles,' I called. 'Charles. Phone.'

'Can you take a message, Dee? I'm busy.'

I ran back and picked up the phone. 'I'm afraid I can't get hold of Mr Blane. Can you leave a message?'

'I'm Sue Ellis from London. Mr Blane asked me to check the dates of birth and marriage of some members of his family. He gave me one name, of someone born in Eighteen forty-two, but I cannot read the writing, nor can I find any trace of a Blane born then.'

'Just a moment.'

I ran to the cupboard where Charles kept his history, found it, ruffled through the pages, impatiently. Then back to the phone again. 'I think,' I said, 'the name you require is Merrick Blane—' I spelled it. 'But the date given here is Eighteen forty-two.'

'Merrick,' said the girl. 'Well, I'll have to check through Eighteen forty-one and Eighteen forty-three, see what I can find. Thank you so much.' The phone went dead.

I left the history on the table, in a hurry to get back to Richard. I ran outside and stopped. The fog was thicker now and I could see no sign of him. 'Richard,' I called. 'Richard.'

There was no answer.

'Richard.' I was frightened now. 'Where are you? Don't hide. Come quickly.'

No answer. The fog swirled around me and I wanted to scream. I ran round the yard out to the road, calling frantically. But there was no reply.

I raced back into the house. 'Charles,' I called. 'Alan. Come down. Please . . .' and I ran out again.

He couldn't be lost, it was impossible. If only I hadn't left him. If only I hadn't answered the phone. If only I'd taken him with me . . .

I was screaming now. 'Charles. Alan. Richard . . .' And the fog was so thick I could not see a yard before me.

It was so quiet. So still. The fog spiralled round my hands, my face, like the fingers of a troll. I edged my way along the wall and came to a door. The dungeon. My fingers scraped along the sides, and it was unlatched.

'No,' I moaned. 'No. Oh, no.'

I swung the door open, and the terrifying blackness met me. 'Richard,' I called, and I had a picture of his mangled body lying at the foot of the stone steps.

Then there came a little cry. 'Dee-Dee.'

He was down there.

I couldn't wait for Charles or Alan, Richard might be dying. I had to go down . . . down there in the blackness.

The thing I had dreaded had come to pass. My nightmare had come true.

CHAPTER FIVE

I cannot describe the horror I felt as I descended the stone steps. I remembered to take the torch, and I needed it, for naturally there was no light in the dungeon. The steps were uneven, and I clung to the walls as I went, saying. 'I'm coming, Richard, I'm coming.'

The steps turned, and I could no longer see the open door. I hoped I'd latched it back firmly. Blackness enveloped me. My nightmare, mine and Mary Dean's.

The steps seemed to go down a long way, and I couldn't hurry for fear of falling. Even greater was the fear that the door would slam shut, that I'd be imprisoned . . . Richard was silent now, there was silence everywhere, it was like the silence of the grave. How horrible to be buried alive.

I was at the bottom, and as I shone my torch around I remember seeing small stalactites hanging from the ceiling. But I could not stop to look at them, even if I wanted to, I was too terrified. 'Richard,' I cried. 'Where are you?'

'Here, Dee-Dee.'

I saw him then, sitting huddled in a corner patiently, and I ran to him and picked him up. 'Are you all right? Are you hurt?' I felt his arms and his poor little legs. He was deathly cold.

'I'm all right, Dee-Dee.'

'Come on, then.' We had to get out. I picked him up and, holding the torch in my right hand, started for the steps. I could not hurry. I had to be careful not to drop Richard, and I could not shine the torch the way I wanted to go. Half-sobbing I felt my way slowly upwards, turned the corner and found Charles and Alan coming to the door.

'Whatever is it?' Charles asked. 'What's going on?'

'Get me out,' I cried. 'Oh, please get me out.'

They came down, gingerly, and it was Alan who pulled me through the door, Charles took Richard from my arms. Then they took us through the clinging fog, back to the warmth of the kitchen.

My teeth were chattering, I was shaking all over. 'Here, drink this,' Charles ordered, and thrust a small glass of brandy into my hand. I swallowed the fiery liquid and gasped. 'Richard. Is he all right?'

Aunt Kitty had fluttered in and was holding him now, crooning. 'Warm some milk,' I said. 'He's frozen.'

Charles went to the cooker, and as he brought the milk I took Richard from Aunt

111

Kitty and let him drink. He was warmer now, and indeed, seemed none the worse for his adventure.

'Whatever happened?' Alan asked. 'We heard you screaming, but didn't know where you were till we saw the dungeon door open.'

'Richard was down there,' I said, my teeth still chattering. 'Someone took him down.'

'Oh, nonsense!' said Charles. 'Who'd do a thing like that?'

'He was down there,' I insisted.

'He must have walked down. The door must have been left open again,' said Charles.

'He couldn't have got down those steps, Charles. You know he can't walk very well. I could hardly get down myself.'

'Children can do amazing things. He could have crawled.'

'No,' I said, obstinately.

'Why not ask him?' said Alan. 'How did you get down the cellar, Richard?'

Richard did not speak.

'I'll take him upstairs, give him a hot bath,' I said. 'We'll talk about this later. Perhaps you'd start dinner, Aunt Kitty, if I'm not down.'

As I took the child to the bathroom I tried to calm myself. Mustn't let Richard see what I felt, mustn't let him see my terror. I ran the water, and peeled off his clothes, placed him in the bath and sat for a moment, trying to relax.

'There now,' I said, as I rubbed him down.

'You did give me a fright. Were you trying to frighten Dee-Dee?'

'Hide and seek,' he said.

I put on his pyjamas and cuddled his warm little body before placing him in bed. He could not have been down the dungeon for more than ten minutes. 'Are you hungry?' I asked.

'Yes.'

'I'll fetch you some nice warm soup. What made you play hide and seek, Richard?'

He said nothing.

I sat on the bed and put my arms around him. 'Did someone take you down there?'

'It's a secret,' he said.

'Ah, but you don't have any secrets from Dee-Dee, do you? I found you, remember. You hid and I found you. But did you get down there yourself?'

'No. He took me.'

'Who? Who, Richard?'

'Don't know.'

'But you must know, darling.'

The child shook his head. 'No. Couldn't see.'

I saw no point in pressing any further. Didn't want to make too big a thing of it. I reflected that he didn't seem unduly upset, that he had never been scared of the dark, and so the dungeon might not be such a terrifying thing to him as it was to me. He did not, after all, suspect that he might have been left there . . . how long? He hadn't had time to be afraid, so I

113

forced myself to laugh and said, 'What a funny game of hide and seek it was. But don't go down there alone, Richard, will you?'

'No.'

'And if you play hide and seek again with someone—come and tell me first, won't you?'

'Yes, Dee-Dee.'

I gave him some of his toys, and went out.

Behind the door I stood, leaning against the wall, my body trembling again. Someone had taken him down the dungeon. Who? How? Charles, Alan and Aunt Kitty had all been upstairs while I used the phone, but any one could have run down the back stairs and up again. Taking a chance, certainly, but it could be done. *It had been done.*

I went down to the kitchen and began to prepare the soup.

Charles said: 'Did you tell Jim Bradshaw about leaving that door open, Alan?'

'Yes. I think so.'

I said. 'The door wasn't open when we went out.'

'Oh, come,' Charles said. 'It's foggy. You wouldn't see the door.'

I tried to think back. Had I noticed the door? I couldn't remember. I began shivering again.

'Sit down,' Charles said. 'You're still shocked.'

'But the soup—'

'Aunt Kitty will prepare it.'

114

I sat down. 'Charles,' I said, 'Richard told me someone carried him down the dungeon.'

'Please, Dee—' That was Alan.

'Do you really mean to say that you think someone from the house went out while you were on the phone, picked Richard up, carried him down there and returned, unseen? Be sensible, Dee,' Charles said.

'It's foggy,' I said. 'No one would see.'

'But why?' Alan asked.

I said nothing. Had someone wanted to get rid of Richard? Or was it done on the spur of the moment by a man who hardly knew what he did? Perhaps wouldn't recall? I said: 'If I hadn't gone down there, he might have died.'

'Is he all right now?' Aunt Kitty asked.

'I'm glad someone is interested,' I flashed, sarcastically. 'Yes, he seems none the worse. And Charles, will you do something about that door?'

'I'll speak to Jim Bradshaw myself.'

'It should be boarded up,' I muttered. 'What's happened once can happen again.'

'Dee, please—'

'He was taken down, he said so.'

'Children do elaborate,' Charles said. But he looked uneasy, his hand trembled slightly.

I turned to Alan. 'You believe me, don't you?' I asked.

He said. 'Well, I don't know, Dee. It seems a bit far-fetched.'

'Aunt Kitty?'

'No one would want to harm a little boy, dear. Now here's the soup. Shall you take it or shall I?'

I faced her silently. It was like battling through a fog, like the fog outside. 'I'll take it,' I almost shouted, jumping up and snatching it from her hands. 'And in future I'll never leave his side, never, not to answer the phone or to get meals or anything.' And I marched away upstairs.

Yet Richard seemed none the worse for his adventure, and I told myself again that he had no idea of the implications. I would say no more about it to him. But I meant to keep my resolve, I would not leave his side, except for the evening meal when he was in bed, and when I went to my own room to sleep.

*   *   *

The first snow fell in December. Light feathery flakes that did not linger, but sent a translucent light into the rooms and intensified the silence. The fogs had gone, and I hoped they would not return. The dungeon episode had affected me more than I'd thought possible, and, coming so soon after the experience in the attic, I found things beginning to prey on my mind. I kept my word and did not let Richard out of my sight, trying at the same time to be completely

116

normal with him. I asked him again about the 'Hide and Seek'. Whose voice had spoken to him? And I got a picture of someone grabbing him from behind, *whispering* 'Let's play hide and seek', then carrying him down. But who would want to harm Richard?

If only I could have talked to someone I'd have felt better, but Mrs Appleby was not back, and the worsening weather conditions made me afraid to attempt the journey to the village. I wondered about Marianne. Had she really gone away or was she, too, perhaps, in the dungeon?

I felt so alone. I saw little of Alan. He was out most weekends, and many week nights, too, working, he whispered to me, and I assumed he meant in the property business. I did not show Charles the paper I'd found in the attic, I did not dare.

So I worked and worried. The cold strengthened, there were patches of ice on the roads, while a bitter east wind tore across the moors under a leaden sky. It was dark at half past three. I felt as though I were living in a perpetual night.

There came a morning mid way through December when the sun came out. I was preparing breakfast, Richard beside me on the rug, and the kitchen was suddenly filled with light. And I knew I had to get out for a day, to escape, that I must risk the car being safe, risk the ice patches, or possible fog. I must get out or I'd go mad.

I put the breakfast on the table, lifted Richard to his chair, helped him to cornflakes. Aunt Kitty was chattering away. 'Soon be Christmas now. We must get a nice turkey . . .'

Resentment at being overworked, of Alan's neglect, of having to watch Richard every minute overwhelmed me. I said: 'I'm going out today, taking Richard. So perhaps you can get your own lunch. And incidentally, if you want any Christmas dinner you'll have to get more help. I've had enough.' And I found tears spilling on my cheeks.

For a moment no one spoke; they all stared at me. Then Charles said: 'Why, Dee, we have been overworking you shamefully. I'm sorry, I just didn't think.'

No, I thought, still resentful. You wouldn't.

'Go out for the day by all means. You don't have to take Richard, Aunt Kitty will look after him.'

'I prefer to take him,' I said, shortly.

Alan said. 'It is a lovely day, I think I'll come, too. We'll go in my car.'

And then the sun was shining in my heart.

Alan went to get the car out, and Charles said: 'Just a minute, Dee, if you wouldn't mind.' I followed him into the study.

He stood, twirling a pen in his hand, looking uncomfortable. 'I know you'll think I'm interfering again,' he said. 'But—do be careful with Alan.'

'Careful? In what way? We're only going out for the day.'

'I know, but I've seen you looking at him, Dee, I know how you feel. I don't want you to get hurt. You are so—vulnerable.'

'Vulnerable, me? Oh, no,' I said. 'I'm as hard as nails. Ask Aunt Meg.'

'I think your Aunt gave you a wrong impression of your character,' Charles said, surprisingly. 'You're not hard at all, Dee. That's why I'm warning you.'

I felt happier suddenly. 'I'll be all right,' I said. 'I'll be careful, I promise.'

As I went out my heart was singing. I had been wrong. Charles didn't object to me as a sister-in-law, I would tell Alan, we could declare our love.

We drove through the village, on to Charby, which was larger, prettier, and had, I noticed, a church, then up to the High Moor. The sun was full out now, there was no mist, it might have been spring. The heather was over now, but the moors still fascinated me, and when we reached a picnic-place I said: 'Let's stop here. Please.'

It was glorious. There was nothing but moor as far as the eye could see. We were alone in the world. I said: 'I must talk to you, Alan.'

And then I told him everything, my feelings on coming to Darrenscar, Mary Dean, the lot. Only one thing I withheld, because Charles had told me in confidence, the fact that he had nearly killed a man once, and was afraid he might do it again. Everything else came pouring out, all my pent-up worries of the last weeks were released. I drew a sobbing breath and waited for him to speak.

'But you don't believe all that?' he asked, incredulously.

'I—I—' I looked around. It did seem crazy here, on the open moor. Inside the house it was different. 'Yes, I suppose I do. Charles does.'

'Oh, Charles!'

'Why don't you two get on, Alan?' I asked. He turned moodily. 'You know, the land business.'

'There's more to it than that, isn't there?'

'Maybe.'

'Why can't you tell me, Alan? Why are there so many secrets at Darrenscar?'

But he evaded giving an answer. Instead he returned to the previous subject. 'What good would it do finding Mary Dean's diary?' he asked.

'I have found one page. And I think the others would tell us something that would help with the present trouble.'

'In what way?'

'To prevent something happening perhaps. A murder.'

'Now you are getting fanciful. Whose murder?'

120

'Have you forgotten Richard in the dungeon?'

'My dear girl, that was not murder.'

'It would have been if I hadn't found him. Made to look like an accident.'

'And you think that if you find out that Stephen Blane killed Mary Dean and her child, this will somehow stop his reincarnation, presumably Charles, from murdering us all in our beds. But how?'

Because, I thought, *I should show it to Charles. Tell him his fears may be realised, tell him he'll have to do something, see a doctor or a clergyman, or I will.*

Aloud I said. 'At least we'd know who to watch.'

'Let's hope it's not Robert who killed her,' Alan said. 'Or that would put me in a spot, wouldn't it? Oh, this is getting us nowhere, Dee. You're wasting your time, anyway. If one of the Blanes did murder her, and we have no proof, and if he took out the pages, then for sure he'd destroy them.'

'But why do that? Why not destroy the whole diary?'

'M'm. You have a point there, I suppose.'

'I think the pages were kept deliberately for some purpose,' I said.

'Such as? One Blane blackmailing the other?' Alan asked. 'I wouldn't put it past them.' He looked bored. 'I still think you're wasting your time.'

I was disappointed. I had hoped so much that Alan would understand.

'Come on,' he said. 'It's cold sitting here. There's a nice little pub in Charby; we'll have a meal.'

We drove away, and I was thinking, leave me alone, Mary Dean. Go away from me. I don't want to be you, I want to be me, Alan's love.

The White Lion was pleasant and warm. Old, with blackened beams and little oak tables. We sat near the window, and after chatting for a time I thought I would raise the other important matter.

'I'm so glad you came,' I told him. 'That you've decided to end the secrecy.'

He smiled. 'It seems a long time since we've been out together.'

'Too long. But Alan, I don't think you need worry any longer about Charles disapproving of—of us. From something he said today I'm sure he doesn't object to me at all.'

'That's big of him.'

'Alan—'

'All right. Sorry. So what did Charles say?'

'Oh—Nothing much,' I evaded. 'But now all you have to do is tell your mother that it's—it's me you love.'

'I wish I didn't.' He was serious suddenly.

'Well, thanks very much.' I drew back, stung.

He laughed then. 'You've bewitched me.'

'Don't say that,' I warned. 'Don't talk about witchcraft.'

'Why not? Think how nice it would be if you could make Charles disappear in a wisp of smoke.'

I smiled. 'You are a fool.'

'But a nice one, H'm?'

'Very nice.' But I had sobered a little, and he noticed this in the way he always did.

'Don't let's rush things,' he said. 'I've rather a lot to worry about at the moment.'

'Your work, you mean? Tell me about it. Is it going well?'

'We've been sounding people out about building those houses on our land. Planning permission would be granted, all we need is the land.'

'Charles would never agree,' I said.

'Then you'll really have to bewitch him, won't you? Because I need that money desperately, Dee. Without it there isn't going to be much of a future for you and me. There isn't going to be much of the future for me. Period.'

I was silent. I hoped he hadn't brought me out in order to persuade Charles to sell the land.

★   ★   ★

Nevertheless, I felt much better for my day out. And that night, for the first time, I opened the

123

book on witchcraft. Glancing through the pages I saw some lines had been marked. *On the Black Art. There was a ritual sacrifice of unbaptised babies . . .*

I sat up in horror. What had Mary Dean written? *I know now what they plan to do . . . such treachery, such wickedness, such baseness, such evil . . .*

Oh no, I thought. Oh no . . .

Slowly I stood up. Slowly, quietly, I made my way to the attic. I sat on the bed, and waited for another revelation. I concentrated on Mary Dean, on her baby . . .

Nothing happened.

It was so cold my fingers were numb. I retraced my steps and went back to my own room.

I opened the book again. Another marked line.

The Death-wish

This is a dangerous mechanism for any but the highly-trained to work. If the sender does not know enough, or if the intended victim has learned the art of self-protection, the death-wish returns, boomerang fashion, to destroy its maker.

So if someone wished me evil I could learn to protect myself. But how? The book did not tell me.

I looked at my watch. Half past twelve. I put the book down. I must study this again.

*　　　*　　　*

That was the last fine day. Sleet was falling in the morning when I went down, there had been a heavy frost, and roads were icy. But Mrs Appleby came back.

It seems that Charles had been remorseful about my working non-stop, and had been to the village to see if he could recruit some help. No one volunteered, but Mrs Appleby's daughter, now seven months pregnant, had been taken to hospital to await the birth, so she offered to come for a time. Charles brought her in, and I could have hugged her.

'It's lovely to see you again,' I said. 'Are you sure you can spare the time?'

'Aye, except for weekends when I shall go to see Mary.'

'And is she all right now?'

'Doctors think so.' Charles went into the study and she looked at me as she took off her coat. 'Been getting you down, has it?' she asked.

'We—ell.' I hardly knew how much to tell her. 'It's this house, I suppose. And the people—they aren't exactly friendly towards one another.'

'I know. You look a bit peaked.' Her glance was concerned. 'You shouldn't have worked so hard.'

'I haven't been doing too much really. It's

just that—I've been worried about Richard.'

'Oh?'

'You see, one day I left him in the yard for a minute while I answered the phone. When I went out I found him in the dungeon.'

'How did he get there?'

'That's what worries me. How could he? He says that someone carried him down, though he couldn't see who it was. Since then I've never dared let him out of my sight. It's been a bit of a strain, I suppose.'

Mrs Appleby didn't laugh, or think I was imagining things. She said: 'He could hardly have got down those steps alone.'

A wave of relief washed over me, to know I was *believed*. 'But who would want to do such a thing?'

'Aye well, who knows,' Mrs Appleby, as always was evasive.

'Marianne, Richard's mother,' I said. 'What *happened*?'

'I wasn't here at the time.' Mrs Appleby made me feel she knew so much more than she would tell me. 'There was a big row, and she—left.'

'I know about that. That she had another man. That Richard isn't Charles' child.'

'He's bound to have enemies,' Mrs Appleby said. 'Because in law he is Charles' child, and his heir.'

For a moment I thought of Alan's words of

yesterday. *How nice it would be if you could make Charles disappear in a wisp of smoke . . . I need that money desperately.* Supposing Richard had been—killed—and Charles was blamed, sent away to prison, to hospital . . . No, don't think that . . . At least it wasn't witchcraft, or was it? How many times had Alan, the unbeliever, mentioned witches yesterday?

'Has the door been bolted up? Padlocked?' asked Mrs Appleby.

'No,' I said.

Her silence was revealing.

'I can't leave Richard,' I said. 'You wouldn't want me to, would you, Mrs Appleby? Anyway, I'll be all right while you're here.'

'I'll come most days till Christmas,' she replied. 'I told Master Charles I would. He's going to fetch me and take me back. After Christmas I can't promise. But no one will go into the yard without me seeing him from the kitchen.'

So for me came respite. I can't explain how much better I felt, with the worry lifted a little from my shoulders. I helped Mrs Appleby, of course, and brought Richard into the kitchen, but I was much easier in my mind. That night I thanked Charles for bringing her back. After all, I thought, he'd hardly be doing something to help if he wanted to get rid of Richard.

Unless something outside himself took over, as he had hinted. The only other alternative was that another person altogether was responsible. And this I wasn't willing to face, that it might be Alan.

★　　★　　★

I wanted to go to York again to buy Christmas presents for Richard. But the weather was worsening; snow and sleet storms and icy roads. It was bitterly cold, and I doubted it would be good for Richard to take him on such a long journey. And I did not intend to leave him, not even with Mrs Appleby. In the end I went to Charles, saying I did not want to travel in the present weather conditions. He suggested I placed an order with one of the big stores, who would be willing to deliver. 'And,' he added, 'send the bill to me.'

'Thank you, Charles,' I said. 'It is good of you.'

So in due course the presents arrived, and I carried them up to my room. I had ordered a tree, and we placed this in the kitchen. 'Really,' I said to Mrs Appleby, 'it is like Christmas, after all.'

We dressed the tree that day, Richard shouting with glee. It was a fine sight, with coloured baubles, tinsel, a fairy right at the top. I stood back to admire my work. 'She's not quite straight,' I said. 'Even with the steps I can't reach it.'

'Get that shepherd's crook from behind the door,' Mrs Appleby said.

I opened the kitchen door, and the cold bit into my throat, taking my breath. The crook was hanging on a nail, and as I brought it in, Mrs Appleby said: 'Made of ash that is, keeps evil away.'

'Really?' I poked the fairy doll into position. 'Do you know any other charms to keep witches away?'

'Oh, aye, lots of 'em. Horseshoes, rowan trees, old keys hung over the door, some herbs.'

'We don't seem to have any of those round here,' I commented.

Mrs Appleby smiled. 'Come summer I'll bring you some lavender,' she said.

I hoped I wouldn't need it before then.

After lunch I took Richard for his nap. He had been excited with the tree, now he was sleepy. I closed the door gently and decided to look in the main bedroom to see if I could find any more of the missing pages.

I went slowly along the silent passage to the room, opened the door quietly and stood stock still. Before the mirror, bathed in the glow of a small lamp, stood a figure. She had her back to me, but her hair was black, she wore the green velvet dress mentioned in Mary Dean's journal, the dress I'd seen before in the trunk. 'Mrs Stephen Blane,' I said, involuntarily, and the figure turned and smiled at me.

129

'Aunt Kitty,' I said. 'How you startled me.'

She patted the dress. 'I am Mrs Stephen—' she began, then, at the incredulous look in my eyes, broke off.

'Your hair—' I said, feebly, and without a word she pulled off the black wig, and stood, a faded old woman.

I left, went back to my own room, sat on the bed, pondering. Then I opened my bag and took out the paper I'd found in the attic, the page of Mary Dean's diary. I thought it was time to show it to Charles.

He was in the study, as always, and I went in, closing the door firmly. Outside, it was getting dark.

I gave him the paper and he read it, frowning. 'Where did you find this?' he asked.

I hesitated. I was still afraid to tell him of my Mary Dean experiences. 'In the attic,' I said, lamely.

'But surely that room's been empty for years?'

'Yes, but there was a loose floorboard. I looked underneath.'

'You did search thoroughly, didn't you? But it still doesn't tell us very much.'

'Only that someone was planning some evil to her and the child, and that she intended to write it out in full. As no doubt she did. There is another paper somewhere, Charles.'

'Yes,' He looked uneasy, almost afraid.

'If I found it, Charles,' I said. 'And we learned that Stephen Blane had killed Mary Dean, what would you do?'

He looked straight ahead. 'I don't really know.' His hand trembled.

I said: 'The pattern is beginning to work again, isn't it? But this time it's Richard, and not a girl . . .' Not yet.

'I had nothing to do with Richard in the dungeon, Dee.'

'Can you swear it wasn't you, Charles?'

'I was in my room.' He jumped up, walked to the window, turned. 'That's all I know. That's all I remember.' His eyes met mine, and they held fear.

I said: 'I've just seen Aunt Kitty dressed in Mrs Stephen Blane's clothes. I understand now what she's been doing all along, pretending to be the grand lady, pretending to be a certain grand lady—Mrs Stephen Blane. Going back into the past. Aunt Kitty's just a foolish old woman.'

'But she is going back, Charles. As if she were a reincarnation, too.'

'Stephen and Robert Blane. Mrs Blane. Mary Dean.' He looked at me, and now his eyes were expressionless. 'Then we're all here, aren't we?'

And I could tell, as I left the room, that he knew about me.

★ ★ ★

How strange it is that such small occurrences can change our whole lives. I remember the day so well. About ten days before Christmas, a crisp, frosty day, snow lay on the High Moor. Richard had had his nap, now we were in the kitchen with Mrs Appleby.

At half past three Charles came in. 'I'm sorry, I just can't run you back today,' he said to Mrs Appleby. 'I wonder if you, Dee, could possibly . . . ?'

'Of course,' I said. 'I'll take Richard.'

The journey to the village took less than half an hour. And if I'd gone straight back . . .

But I didn't. I decided to call in the corner shop, wondering if I'd learn anything else about Darrenscar.

Mrs Briggs was behind the counter, and there was another woman in the shop, a thin, dark-haired woman who stared at me suspiciously. Mrs Briggs smiled at me. 'How's things at Darrenscar?' she asked.

'Fine,' I said. 'Just fine.'

The other woman sniffed. 'How you can stay there after all that's happened—' she began.

I wondered if she'd heard about Richard and the dungeon. If she could perhaps throw some light on the mystery. I asked: 'What happenings do you mean?'

'You don't *know*?' The woman sniffed again. 'You don't know about Marianne?'

132

An icy finger crept down my spine. 'Marianne?' I echoed, foolishly. Mrs Briggs said nothing, her face seemed to loom in the air before me, her eyes watchful.

'Charles turned her out,' the woman said. 'Because she was having a love affair. She drove off in the car and was killed.'

'Oh, no,' I said. 'Oh, *no!*'

'It's true.' The woman seemed almost to be enjoying herself. 'She was having an affair with young Alan.'

CHAPTER SIX

I don't know how I got back to Darrenscar. I remember parking the car and taking Richard to the study. I remember switching on the lamp because it was so dark. Then I just sat. Richard came to me with a little whimper. 'Dee-Dee.' And I lifted him on my lap and held him close. I wondered why it had never occurred to me that Alan was involved. I had been searching for a cause of the trouble between the cousins, I knew it must be something serious. But I had had a picture of Marianne leaving to join another man, some vague creature from far away. I realised now I should have known it all along. How could she have an affair with another man, living in this isolated spot? Alan was here . . . Alan, my love . . .

How could he let her go away alone?

I was in a limbo of pain, and I wanted to succumb to it utterly, to go to my room and lie in the darkness, never do anything again. Instead I had to carry on with the ordinary mundane things of life, put dinner on the table, wash up . . . I had to take Richard to bed . . .

He knew something was wrong. He looked up into my face, puzzled. 'Have you a pain?' he asked.

'A little one,' I said. 'It will be better soon.'

But it wouldn't. Not soon, maybe not ever . . .

I carried Richard into the kitchen, and saw it was six o'clock. 'Time for your supper,' I said, and moved to the cooker.

Aunt Kitty came in, chattering away as usual. I could have screamed. I don't think I heard a word she said, till she came close to me and asked: 'Is something wrong, Dee?'

'Of course not,' I replied shortly. 'What could be wrong?'

'How should I know? Maybe you're getting tired of Darrenscar.'

'Come, Richard,' I said. 'Up to bed.'

He snuggled down, and I read him a little story, as I always did. I kissed him goodnight, and went to the window. The High Moor was white, the cold seemed a living thing, freezing everything in its clutches. Hastily I drew the curtains and went down.

Dinner was unreal. I put the meal on the table, I even ate some of it, for I did not want to draw attention to myself. I heard Charles say he was worried about the worsening weather conditions. 'You'll have to bring the sheep down, Alan,' he said. 'Either to Jim's, or the back grazing here.'

Then dinner was over—had any meal ever lasted so long? Alan went to his room, as did Aunt Kitty. Charles lingered for a moment, and as I went to the sink, said: 'Don't you mind being left here alone? Why don't you leave the dishes till morning?'

'No,' I said. 'I'd rather do them now. I don't mind being alone.'

I wanted to be alone. Later, I had to confront Alan.

Even so, I waited awhile, plucking up my courage. Then I went towards his room and knocked quietly. I thought how odd it was that after all his pleadings I should be going to him—for this.

He opened the door and smiled. 'Dee,' he breathed. 'Come in.'

I went inside, and the door was closed. He looked at me and his smile faded a little. 'What is it?' he asked.

'Marianne,' I said.

He drew in his breath. 'So—you know.'

Even to this last minute I'd hoped it wasn't

true. 'I know,' I said.

'Sit down. We must talk.'

I sat in an armchair, and he faced me. 'Why didn't you tell me?' I asked.

'How could I, Dee? Be reasonable. What would you have thought?'

'What I'm thinking now, I expect,' I said.

'It was just a brief affair. All right, I was crazy, but I was only nineteen. What fellow would resist what is offered to him?'

'You just couldn't resist the temptation?' My voice was sarcastic, hurting, I wanted to hurt him.

'Well, I'm only human, I suppose.'

'I think I can understand all that,' I said, carefully. 'But what about Richard? To let her be sent away, alone . . . Why, Alan? Because you had to wait for your inheritance?'

'You don't know what happened,' and now his face had the little boy look I loved so well. 'Charles found out, he raised hell. He nearly killed me.'

I nearly killed a man once. Dear God.

'If Jim Bradshaw hadn't come in . . . I had to go to hospital.'

I closed my eyes.

'When I came home Marianne had gone. Charles told her to go.'

'And didn't he tell you to go, too?'

Alan rumpled his hair. 'Well, there was my mother . . . Anyway, fellows do have affairs,

136

you know.'

'Not usually with their cousin's wife in his house.'

'It is my home, too. Though I'm not trying to excuse myself.'

'You should have gone with her, Alan. And then—there is Richard.' I drew a painful breath. 'I can't understand why you ignore the child. You never talk to him. Why?'

He shrugged, turning away. 'I don't know. Guilt, I suppose.'

'Couldn't you forget your guilt for the sake of the boy?'

'Be realistic, Dee. How can I go around flaunting the boy as my own? If he *is* mine.'

'And that's a typical masculine remark if I ever heard one. No wonder Charles warned me about you. Oh, no wonder!' I was almost crying now, and I didn't want to cry, didn't want to let him see he had the power to hurt me.

He said: 'I don't suppose you care for me any longer, after all this?'

I wanted to say, No, I hate you. I wanted to scream, Get away from me, as he came closer. I couldn't. The same fascination held me as always. I thought drearily, it's like a magic spell, I can't get free . . .

What would have happened I don't know, but the door opened suddenly and Aunt Kitty came in. Alan and I jumped apart. Aunt Kitty said: 'I just came to have a chat, dear. I didn't

137

know you weren't alone.'

'I'm going now,' I said. 'Goodnight.'

I went out, stopped, startled, Charles was outside his door, watching me.

I ignored him, went in my room, prepared wearily for bed. It was not until I went to switch out the light that I noticed that the witchcraft book was no longer there. I looked in the drawers, on the floor. Nothing. It had disappeared completely.

* * *

Mrs Appleby offered to come on Christmas Eve, but I would not hear of it. The roads were bad, there was snow and heavy frost, I felt it was too much to ask. 'I'll be all right,' I told her. 'Wait until the New Year. Maybe the snow will be gone then,'

'If you're sure—' she said. 'I would be relieved. My daughter hasn't been well again, I must try to see her.'

'I'm quite sure,' I said. 'Now have a very happy Christmas, and thank you for all your help.'

Even so, she lingered in the doorway and gave me a searching look. But I put on a smile, and showed a confidence I was far from feeling. Then Charles came to take her home, and I waved goodbye.

It was the last time I'd see her for a long

time.

I turned back to Richard. I was determined to give him a happy time at Christmas, my own feelings must be subordinated to this. In truth, the first bitter pain had become a dull ache, a sad lonely feeling that was always with me. I had known that Alan was weak; most of his problem stemmed, I thought, from this. But his disregard for Richard and Marianne seemed quite callous. He was dominated by his mother, Charles had always had a down on him . . . What had Charles said once about Alan some day wanting his revenge?

And then I began to think about the other thing, which I'd ignored in my first overwhelming pain. Marianne had been killed, driving away from Darrenscar. Charles had told her to go. Was this, too, part of the gipsy's curse? And who would be next?

I put the thoughts out of my mind. There must be no trouble at Christmas. On that I was determined.

I put Richard to bed fairly early on Christmas Eve. He was thrilled and excited as all children are. 'Will Father Christmas really come?' he asked.

'Of course,' I said. 'Go to sleep now, and in the morning there'll be all those lovely presents.'

He closed his eyes trustingly.

Back downstairs I checked over the supplies.

Mrs Appleby and I had made mince-pies and a cake. The puddings had been bought. The turkey, plucked, hung in the pantry.

'Couldn't we light a fire in the sitting-room tomorrow?' I asked. 'There's that marvellous open fireplace, and with logs—'

'Of course,' Charles said. 'I have to go to the farm tonight.'

I looked at him. His face was drawn, he seemed tired. I knew he'd been rushing his book, wanting to get it away, to get paid, he told me wryly. 'Can't Alan go to the farm?' I asked. 'It's his job.'

Alan put down the apple he was eating and gave me a glance that held surprise and a certain sullenness. But he said, easily enough. 'OK. I'll go.'

'Just see that the sheep are all right,' Charles said. 'Most of them are in lamb. Where are they, at the back of Bradshaw's?'

Alan muttered what sounded like an affirmative, and in ten minutes we heard the sound of the Landrover being driven away. Aunt Kitty went to her room, murmuring something about preparing for the party tomorrow. Charles and I were left alone. I looked out at the snowy landscape and switched on the radio.

A boy's choir was singing a carol, and as the pure sound cascaded into the room Charles gave a little sigh. 'It is really Christmassy,' he said. 'I must thank you, Dee. It's been a long time—'

He looked tired, and I would have felt sorry for him if it hadn't been for the thought of Marianne, sent away, driving to her death . . . 'You can relax,' I said, curtly.

'I must get some money,' he muttered. 'If only the weather would improve . . . We must sell those lambs.'

'I'm sure it will be better after Christmas,' I said.

How little we know.

Alan returned and said everything was under control, no need to worry. I crept up to Richard's room and filled his stocking, heaped the presents around the bed, and went to bed myself, to sleep dreamlessly.

Christmas morning was a happy time for Richard. He was too impatient even to let me dress him. Laughing, I carried him downstairs to where Charles had already lit a fire in the sitting-room, and was pleased to see the two of them together playing with the train set.

I cooked the turkey, for we planned to have dinner at one o'clock for Richard's benefit, and everything went off well. The party was planned for the afternoon, with fruit and mince-pies, and the Christmas cake. I had bought crackers, and paper hats, and for once I was glad of Aunt Kitty. She did not do much to help me, she spent the whole afternoon getting ready, and emerged clad in the green velvet dress of Mrs Blane's. But it did not affect me now, and while Charles was silent, and Alan morose, Aunt Kitty pulled crackers and wore a paper hat and suggested games to play. Richard enjoyed himself tremendously, and when he finally went to bed he hugged me and kissed me, and I felt it had all been worthwhile.

*   *   *

Yet two days later it was as though Christmas had never been. Richard still had his toys, and was happy, but Charles had a sudden call from his publishers. Could he please let them have the book a month earlier than he'd promised? He returned to the study, still looking strained.

'I just won't have time to get to the farm,' he told Alan. 'You'll see to everything, won't you?'

'I will,' Alan promised.

The weather seemed to be getting colder, if that were possible. Charles had cleared the frozen snow from the yard to get to Aunt Kitty's chickens in the stable, and indeed to get to the road. Driving conditions were bad, and I wondered if it were necessary for Alan to go all the way to York every day. But of course, he'd told me he needed money desperately.

There was a heavy fall of snow on New Year's Eve, the temperature dropped to twenty degrees of frost. Alan was out, Aunt Kitty in her room. Charles came out of the study and dropped into an arm chair. 'The book's finished,' he said.

'Good.'

He leaned back, and I stared at him, a million thoughts throbbing through my brain, bringing all the hidden fears to the surface. And I felt there were things I had to know, about Marianne, her death, her love . . . I said: 'Tell me about Marianne.'

His head jerked up. 'What?'

'I heard it in the village,' I said. 'About she and Alan, and you . . . Did you send her to her death, Charles?'

'I don't remember.' His voice was low, almost a whisper.

Outside, darkness began to close round the windows, a flurry of snow fell over the panes. Charles began talking, almost compulsively, as if it were something he repeatedly went over in his mind, as if it were a relief to say it all aloud.

'Things had been strained between us for some time,' he said. 'She was cold to me. I thought it was because of the baby, or perhaps I neglected her as I was overworked . . . I never dreamed there was anyone else. How could there be? I loved her fiercely, possessively, intensely . . .'

'Perhaps,' I said, 'you were too fierce, Charles. Marianne looked to be a gentle girl from the photograph.' *Too gentle for the harsh world of Darrenscar.*

'I gave her all the love I'd been denied,' he went on. 'And when I learned she'd turned to Alan . . . Alan—' he choked.

'Maybe she found him undemanding,' I suggested. And indeed, I felt I could see it all. Gentle Marianne, afraid of her stern, fierce husband, longing for kindness . . . I asked: 'How did you find out?'

'I went into her room one evening . . . we had had separate rooms since Richard was born. I caught them together. And then I went a little mad, I think. I hardly remember what happened. I remember shouting Richard wasn't mine—'

'And what did Marianne say to that?'

'She said he was.'

'And then—?'

'I remember hitting Alan. And that's all. I didn't know Marianne had gone. Not till later, when they came to tell me . . . to tell me that she had crashed the car . . .' He gave a shuddering sigh.

'But—' I began, and he interrupted.

'Don't you see?' he said, and his voice was hoarse. 'I killed her, too. Didn't I?' And he walked out of the room.

*   *   *

For another couple of weeks we went on as usual. And then the blizzard came.

144

It had been snowing on and off since December. The sky was full of snow. Even so, the blizzard took us by surprise.

It was Friday, I remember. It had been snowing all day, and was bitterly cold outside. Charles was working in his study. He asked Alan about the sheep. 'I'll go down myself tomorrow,' he said. But he couldn't.

It snowed all night. I remember once waking to see the heavy flakes falling, and the room lit with the same unearthly brilliance. But I didn't get out of bed.

We woke in the morning to find snow up to the tops of the kitchen windows, and drifts over the road up to ten feet deep.

I had never known anything like it. To go down in the morning and find yourself snowed in was frightening. My fear must have showed, for Charles said: 'Don't worry, Dee, it's happened before. We'll clear it after breakfast.'

He went to the phone while I made hot tea and eggs and bacon. 'Damn,' he said. 'The phone's dead. I'm worried about the sheep. Which field did you put them in, Alan?'

Alan didn't answer. He was staring at the window.

Charles said sharply, 'Alan. You did bring them down? They are at Jim's?'

Alan said: 'No.'

'What do you mean, no?' Charles had jumped to his feet, overturning the chair. 'You've been going to the farm . . .'

'Oh hell, Charles, how could I find them in this bitter cold? I can't really work the dogs—'

'My God,' Charles said,. 'They must be buried. The lambs will die.'

'They'll be all right,' Alan said, uncertainly. 'They'll shelter—'

'Shelter where?' Charles asked, curtly. 'If you'd brought them down here, at the back of the house, we could have got to them.' He stood up. 'Come on, let's clear the snow. I'll see if I can get through.'

The door opened inwards and in the doorway was a wall of frozen snow. The men hacked it down, and went outside with shovels. I asked if I could help and they agreed. I put on every woolly I possessed, but the cold was a tangible thing, you could almost see it as it hit you in the chest, on the face. Great drifts of snow lay against the side of the house where the kitchen window was, and against the stables. Ironically, the dungeon door was clear.

We dug round the window, and it was hard, tiring work. I had never realised that such a soft substance as snow could be so hard to remove. 'Stables next,' said Charles.

We worked for hours, and cleared most of the yard. Then Charles went towards the gate.

'That's a waste of time,' Alan said. 'We'll need a digger.' The drifts were deep here, the gate was covered.

146

I walked as far as I could and stared. There was nothing anywhere but snow, great hills and folds, dazzling in the light. The road to the village was completely blocked, drifts lay in strange shapes, and everywhere was the silence, as if the world was dead.

'The village must be cut off,' Alan said.

'What will they do?' I asked, my teeth chattering.

'Don't worry, they'll get through, sooner or later. There'll be a snow plough.'

Alan and I went indoors, leaving Charles in the yard. 'When will they repair the phone?' I asked.

'Soon as they can get to it. If it's an underground cable—'

He broke off as Charles came in, stamping his feet against the cold. 'Dee,' Charles said. 'Would you feed the chickens? The yard's too slippery for Aunt Kitty.'

I nodded, and took the food, prepared in a saucepan. Great icicles hung over the stable, breaking off with a sharp snap as I opened the door. I peered into the gloom inside. It was quite warm in here, there was plenty of straw, the birds were sitting on it, but they seemed uneasy, restless, and made no move to come for the food. I thought there was a strange smell, too, but perhaps chickens did smell . . .

I took a step forward. And then I saw it. I dropped the saucepan and screamed, running indoors, gasping, choking . . . 'The black cockerel,' I gulped. 'Hanging from the ceiling, upside down . . . its throat cut—'

'Jesus,' said Alan, and he and Charles raced outside. Aunt Kitty followed them to the doorway and stood, looking out.

'Come back, Aunt Kitty,' I said. 'Shut the door, keep it out . . . *please*' My voice rose, cracked.

She did as I asked. 'Horrible,' she said. 'It's starting again. Horrible things.'

I sat down, trembling, and it seemed a long time before the men returned, silent, thoughtful. But I couldn't let it go, I was horrified, scared. 'Who did it?' I shouted. 'No one could have got in.' *Only you, Charles. You were outside, alone.*

'My poor chickens,' said Aunt Kitty, seeming on the verge of tears. 'What did you do with it?'

'Buried it under the snow. What else could we do?' Charles asked.

'But who—?' I began.

'Someone's idea of a joke, maybe,' Alan said.

Pretty poor joke, I thought.

'Leave it now,' Charles said. 'We have too much to worry about without that.'

We sat silent. And it began to snow again.

When the early darkness fell I got up to switch on the light. Nothing happened.

I tried the cooker, and that was working, as was the central heating.

'That's odd,' said Charles. 'Must be a fuse.'

He went to the fuse box in the hall, and was away a long time, while the shadows deepened and the white world outside lay under a dark sky. He returned, puzzled, 'Nothing wrong there,' he said. 'The hobgoblins must be at work. Well, we'll just have to have candles, we always keep a good stock in.'

He foraged in the cupboard and emerged with several large candles and lit them. Flickering, they gave an eerie look to the usually bright kitchen.

I prepared dinner, but none of us felt much like eating. We sat in the light of the flickering candles while shadows quivered over the ceiling, strange shapes that seemed to come near, and recede, weird shapes with long beckoning fingers.

That night when I went to bed the book on witchcraft was back by my bed. I opened it and it fell open at a marked page. I read with horror:

A black cock is used in the blood sacrifice rites of the Black Mass. I dropped the book as if it were the devil himself. My horror mounted. I blew out the candle and tried to sleep. It was still snowing.

★   ★   ★

We heard on the local radio that the village was

cut off, that a snow plough was trying to get through, but with no success. Drifts lay too high over the road. We heard that the whole country had suffered, that farmers were worried about their sheep. Charles went out to look at the possibility of getting out, but the road was impassable. He went back to the study and shut himself in.

Alan fed the chickens, and reported they were all right. I sat with Richard, and tried to act as though nothing was wrong. They'll get through tomorrow, I thought, we'll be rescued. I went to look at our stores. The big freezer was full, the shelves were loaded with tins and preserves, we had dried milk and eggs and bread. We certainly wouldn't starve.

I lit the candles and wondered vaguely why they flickered so much when there was no apparent current of air. I prepared dinner, and we watched the news on television. There was a picture of a farmer digging out sheep, two alive, one dead.

I waited anxiously for the weather forecast. 'The worst winter for many years,' said the announcer. 'There is no sign of a thaw. More snow is on the way.'

It snowed again that night. And I realised that Aunt Kitty's words were true. My nightmare had come true. I was trapped at Darrenscar, just as I had known I would be.

Looking back, I remember little of the days.

Life fell into a pattern. It snowed, and we cleared the yard, great icicles hung over the stable door. Some black birds hovered in the sky, and Charles said they were crows. I thought they looked like vultures.

It was the nights that filled me with fear. On the third night I took my candle to the bedroom. The witchcraft book, which I had left lying on the floor, had been placed on the bed, opened to the title page where the name Stephen Blane was written. I remembered it well.

But now, beneath the name, and in the same bold handwriting, were the words: *DRAW DOWN THE DARK MOON*.

I gasped. What did it mean?

I wished I'd never brought the book here in the first place. I wanted to get rid of it, but no power on earth could have persuaded me to walk downstairs to the dustbin through the dark passages with only the light of a candle. And we had no fire. If I placed it in the dustbin would it be returned again?

Gingerly I put the book in the drawer, blew out the flickering candle and closed my eyes tight, trying vainly to shut out the fears and terrors of the night.

The fourth night was even more frightening. I went to bed and drew back the curtains. I would not, I thought, be dependent on candlelight with its strange shadows. I gazed for a moment at the lifeless world of snow. Then I jumped into bed.

A strange blue light filled the room, and I was puzzled. Could it be reflection from the snow? Again I went to the window, and saw the trees around the house, snow-laden, were waving to and fro. And yet there was no breath of wind. The night was clear, there were even a few stars.

I felt very cold. So cold that I thought the central heating had failed, and went to the radiator. It was full on, hot. Shivering, I stood close to it, watching the waving trees in the dead world. The blue light intensified.

With a gasp of terror I drew the curtains again. The light was still there. I flung myself into bed and covered my face, shivering.

It was a long time before I slept.

*   *   *

In the morning I prepared breakfast and wondered if the others had seen anything odd. But no one mentioned it if they had. We listened to the weather forecasts of more snow, of driving accidents, of people buried alive in cars. There was no sign of a thaw.

'I think,' Charles said, heavily, 'it will be quite a time before they can get to us.'

Alan shrugged carelessly, and Charles rounded on him. 'I suppose Jim Bradshaw thinks you brought our sheep down here. Well, doesn't he? Did you tell him that?'

'I suppose so,' Alan said.

Charles groaned, and I thought of the sheep, huddled together somewhere, buried, frozen . . .

I went up to Richard, sitting in bed, waiting for me. His cuddly toy was on the bed, books and other toys were scattered aorund his room. 'Come, my love,' I said. 'Let's get you dressed.'

'Can we go out today, Dee-Dee?'

'I don't think so, Richard, it's much too cold. And the yard is frozen. 'Fraid we'll have to be stay-at-homes.'

'I'm going out,' he said.

'Are you?' I smiled, 'And where do you think you're going?'

'Hide and seek,' he said.

'What?' For a moment I didn't understand.

'You said no secrets, Dee-Dee. Hide and seek again.'

And then my smile froze as I remembered what hide and seek had meant. The dungeon.

I strove to hide my fears. 'You mean you'd like to play again?'

'We are going to play. He said so.'

'Who said?' My voice seemed to waver.

'Don't know. He came last night and whispered. "We're going to play hide-and-seek." You said tell you, Dee-Dee.'

'That's right. What did you say to him?'

'I said "I want Dee-Dee". And he went.'

'You didn't see who it was?' Stupid question.

'No. It was dark.'

'Perhaps you dreamed it . . . ?' But he shook his head.

I wondered what to do. Tell the others? They hadn't believed me before, why should they now? At least, two wouldn't believe me, the others . . . ? Who had killed the black cockerel? Someone was practising witchcraft. To invoke what? To call on evil spirits? . . . Was it Charles . . . ?

We were cut off from the world. If anything happened I could not get help. I could not ring, the phone was still dead. I could not get out. If Richard were found wandering in the snow no one would suspect foul play—except me.

My own life was in danger. The strange manifestations I had seen were not imagination, or tricks of the lights, they were tricks of witchcraft, done deliberately—to me.

Would the police find it odd when they finally got to us and found a girl and a child dead? If they were in the dungeon, yes, but if they had been taken out, placed in the snow, what proof would they have of murder? Just another couple of casualties to add to the sheep and the people in cars . . .

Why me?

I knew why. I remembered Charles' words. Mrs Blane, Stephen and Robert Blane, Mary

Dean. We're all here. Again.

The pattern was repeating itself, and I knew of no way of breaking it.

All I could do was protect Richard as best I could.

I took him downstairs and gave him breakfast. I had a violent headache, unusual for me, and as I turned round the room swum giddily. Aunt Kitty said: 'Aren't you well, Dee?'

'Just a headache,' I muttered.

'Why don't you take an aspirin?'

'Thanks, I will.'

'Just sit down for a while. I'll wash up.'

She moved to the sink, chatting the while. 'I'm glad to be doing something, it's so bad being stuck in like this. Not that I go out much, but at least we can go if we want to. Now we're completely cut off.'

I said nothing.

'Of course, we've had bad winters before. I remember in Eighteen eighty-three, that was a terrible winter—'

I wanted to shout 'Stop it. How can you remember Eighteen eighty-three?' But I didn't say the words. A thought had come to me. Why did Aunt Kitty dress in Mrs Stephen's clothes, act the grand lady? Did she really go back into the past? If so, how much did she know?

I said: 'Who killed Mary Dean?'

She turned. 'Why, Stephen Blane, of course.

You look white, Dee. Maybe you should go and lie down.'

'I'm all right,' I said.

My head ached all day. I wondered what to do about Richard when he went to bed. Surely no one in their right mind would take a child out in the night . . . But was I dealing with someone who wasn't in their right mind . . . ?

I decided to sleep in Richard's room, lock the door. That was the only way. That way we'd be safe.

Aunt Kitty helped with the lunch and dinner, and I was grateful. I asked her if she'd put the dinner out, I'd take Richard to bed and myself, too. I didn't want any food.

'Yes, I'll do that, dear. Do you want something to make you sleep?'

'No thanks, I'll be fine.'

I hoped I would. I couldn't afford to be ill. Not now.

I gave Richard his bath and put him to bed. 'Now,' I said. 'How would you like it if Dee-Dee stayed with you?'

'All night?'

'Yes, it's cold in my room. But you must go to sleep. No talking.'

'Night-night.' He closed his eyes obediently.

When I saw he slept I fetched my things from my room, undressed, and went to lock the door. I stopped. There was no key.

I slipped out again, looked in the other doors.

None had keys. Well, it was an old house, no doubt they'd been lost over the years. So what to do?

I must push something behind the door. There was a small chest of drawers, not too heavy, but enough at least to wake me if an intruder decided to come in. I heaved it along, and jumped into bed.

I was dreaming. I was Mary Dean again, in the dungeon, and Richard was with me, three-year-old Richard. Someone had locked us in, and was hammering the door to keep it shut. Bang, bang, bang, went the hammer . . .

I woke, and someone was banging the door on the chest, trying to get in.

'Who is it?' I called.

'It's only me—Aunt Kitty. It's nine o'clock.'

Nine o'clock! I jumped out of bed, pulled back the curtains. Richard was wide awake. 'Good heavens, I've overslept,' I said.

'It doesn't matter. But I brought you a cup of tea. I went to your room, but you weren't there, so I guessed you were here. Are you feeling better?'

'Yes, I'm fine. Just a minute.'

I pulled the chest away and took the tea. 'I'll be down in a minute,' I promised.

I hastily dressed, and just as hastily dressed Richard. We would go down together.

The others were just finishing breakfast as we went in. 'Sorry I'm late,' I said.

'What on earth was that banging?' Charles asked.

'Oh, it was me, trying to get in,' Aunt Kitty said.

'Trying to get in where, for God's sake?' Charles' temper was fraying.

'I pushed a chest behind the door,' I said.

'Good God, whatever for?' Charles stared, and Alan said with a smile. 'No one's going to break in, Dee. No one can get within two miles of us.'

They all stared at me, and I felt a fool. I said, lamely. 'I don't know. I felt a little scared, I suppose. It's all this—' and I flung my hand out, vaguely.

'Are you sure you're all right?' Charles asked. 'You were ill yesterday.'

'I'm better now.'

'Yes, but, pushing a chest behind the door was a silly thing to do. If you had been ill no one could have got in the room to you.'

'I'm not ill, Charles.'

'Well, don't do it again. I've enough to worry about as it is, without hysterical females acting up.'

He went out, slamming the door.

★ ★ ★

In the afternoon I took Richard for his nap, but I didn't leave him. I had first fetched the book on witchcraft, for I badly wanted to learn something about the strange manifestations I had seen, and it wasn't quite so frightening reading it in daylight. I opened the book to the words, *Draw Down the Dark Moon*, then leafed through the pages, and began to read.

Witchcraft, the oldest religion in the world. The Druids. The coming of Christianity and the persecutions of the middle ages. There were details of famous trials, of men in high places, of black witches, lovers of evil, and white witches who blessed and healed. Fertility rites. The witches sabbats, Hallowe'en, Candlemas, May Eve and Lammas.

It was a fallacy to think that witches were bent old crones. Many young people have delved into witchcraft, and as many men as women. Charles had told her that . . .

Richard was beginning to stir, and I closed the book and put it in a drawer. If only I knew what Mary Dean had written before she died . . . If only I could remember . . . But however much I concentrated nothing came to me.

I took Richard's hand and went to the big front bedroom. The room where Stephen Blane had slept, where Geoffrey Blane had taken the gipsy. The huge four-poster stood massively in the centre; I shivered as I looked at it. I did not draw back the curtains, but switched on the light and started my search. Richard played happily on the floor with one of his toys.

I had already looked through the bureau. Now I opened the chests, pulled out the clothes, shook them all, put them back. I opened drawers, tried to find secret hiding places, even looked on the floor for loose boards, and under the heavy mattress on the big bed.

There was nothing.

It was cold, for the heating was not on in this room, so I took Richard downstairs. I had to decide what I was going to do about tonight.

My head ached and this worried me. But I prepared dinner, though I did not take Richard to bed. As we sat down Charles raised his eyebrows. 'Isn't it his bedtime?' he asked.

'I've decided to let him sit up for dinner,' I said. 'Then I shall to go bed, too.'

'Don't you feel well?' Charles looked at me, and in the candlelight I could not tell if his expression was concerned or malevolent.

I said, 'I've decided to sleep in Richard's room again. And I shall push the chest by the door as there is no key.'

'But why?' Alan asked.

'Because Richard had a strange dream. About the dungeon.'

'Oh, Dee. Not that again.' Alan had his bored look.

'I don't like to think of you being barricaded in,' Charles said. 'If you were ill we couldn't get in to you.'

That was twice he'd said that.

'We could,' Alan contradicted. 'If the chest can be moved by Dee, then obviously we could push it away again if necessary.'

That was a thought. But at least I'd hear it.

Nothing more was said, so I took Richard to bed. The washing up could wait till morning, I thought callously, or Aunt Kitty could do it. Or Alan for that matter, now he was at home all day.

'You needn't wake me,' I told Aunt Kitty. 'I'll be down as usual.'

But I wasn't. When I woke, light was streaming through the curtains, and Richard was sitting beside me talking to his toys. I looked at my clock. Half past ten.

I jumped out of bed, feeling heavy, as though I'd been drugged. I dressed Richard, and we went down. The kitchen was empty.

We were eating breakfast when Charles came in. 'I thought I heard you,' he said. 'We didn't wake you. How are you?'

'I can't understand why I'm oversleeping like this,' I said. 'I've never done it before.'

'Have you an alarm clock?'

'Yes, a small travelling clock. I sleep through it.'

'You're not worrying about us being cut off here, are you?'

'I don't like it,' I said.

'We have plenty of food; they'll get through

161

eventually.'

'But how long will it be, Charles?'

'I don't know, Dee. We have been snowed in before, that's why we always keep ourselves well-stocked. They know that in the village, they know we'll be all right. But they'll get through as soon as they can'

'Supposing something happened?' I muttered.

'Such as what?'

'Such as something terrible. You told me about all this, Charles, and I tell you there have been strange happenings.'

'What happenings?'

'There was a blue light in my room, the night before I went to Richard.'

'Reflection from the snow, no doubt.'

'No, it wasn't. And then—' I was about to say the trees were waving, the candles flickered, but stopped. Trees did wave, candles did flicker. 'What about the dead cockerel?' I asked.

'I know that was pretty nasty, but I didn't want to keep talking about it.'

'You know what it was, Charles?' My voice was rising, hysterically. 'You know what it was done for?'

'Dee, look, it was just a joke. It's all my fault for telling you about the history. Now you're letting it prey on your mind.'

'Charles, there's nothing wrong with my

162

mind.'

'I didn't say there was, I just meant you were letting it all get you down a bit. You'll feel better when the snow's gone and we can get out again.'

'I hope so,' I muttered. 'And anyway, why am I sleeping so heavily?'

'Are you taking sleeping pills?'

'No, though I feel as though I am.'

'Take it easy,' Charles said. 'Try not to worry.'

He went out again, and I wondered if he were genuinely sympathetic, or if he wanted it to appear that I was going out of my mind.

Maybe I am, I thought, fearfully. Maybe I'm imagining all this . . .

If only I could find some proof . . . This afternoon, I thought, I'll search Charles' room. I know it isn't a nice thing to do, but maybe there'll be something . . . Mary Dean's paper . . .

But I didn't do anything after all. I took Richard for his nap and fell asleep beside him. And when I woke I knew there was something wrong with me. My head felt heavy, confused, I was giddy.

Was someone putting something in my food? How could they when I prepared it myself? Yet we were all in the kitchen, we all walked near the cooker, the plates. Alan spent more time here than ever I'd known him to do; he had washed up several times lately, saying he wanted to help me . . .

It was Saturday before I felt able to search Charles' room, and we had been prisoners for a week.

I took the Hoover upstairs, Richard with me, and opened Charles' door, halting on the threshold, wondering if I'd find a little wax image somewhere. I went inside, to the chest of drawers, rummaged through, feeling guilty, trying not to look at anything that was not the evidence I wanted. Over to the wardrobe, the bedside cabinet, the table underneath the window.

There was nothing.

On Sunday I felt really ill, I could not work at all. I had a violent headache, I could not think clearly. The others were concerned, and their faces loomed at me out of a candlelit gloom, for there'd been no light outside almost all day. The snow lay, fold upon fold, but I no longer thought it was beautiful. It was menacing.

'Why don't you go to bed, Dee?' Charles asked.

But I wanted to stay with Richard, to watch the kitchen.

Two more days passed, and I grew weaker. I made an effort to talk to Alan one day when we were alone, but I could no longer marshall my thoughts in sequence. I said: 'I think someone's trying to poison me.'

'Oh, Dee.' He looked alarmed. 'You mustn't think things like that. Dee, what has upset you? Was it me?'

'No,' I said. 'At least, I don't think so. It could be you, couldn't it? Giving me the death-wish.'

He looked more alarmed than ever.

'Be—be careful,' I said. 'Because if I protect myself, it will rebound on you and destroy you.'

I hadn't meant to say that at all.

I took Richard to bed early and sat, thinking. They thought I was going crazy. Aunt Kitty fluttered around me until I could have screamed. Charles wished he could get a doctor. He even went out with a shovel in a vain attempt to hack his way out, but it was hopeless. The drifts lay implacably over the road. Night after night the newscaster said: 'There is no sign of a thaw.'

I wondered what my enemy, the evil-lover, was planning to do. Send me mad? Make me so ill that Richard could disappear without trace . . . ? Blame me for it? While of unsound mind?

On Tuesday, the night was clear, and the moon rose. Richard was sleeping, and I went to the window. The massive piles of snow lay whitely, and I saw the moon was full.

But it was not till the next afternoon that the change came to me. Richard had had his nap, and he woke to see me lying on the bed. He jumped up. 'Dee-Dee,' he said. 'Why?'

'Yes, Richard?' I said, hastily.

'Why are you—' he hesitated, trying to frame his words. 'Why are you sick, Dee-Dee?'

'I'm not sick, Richard. Just tired.'

'Dee-Dee. Are you going away?'

'Why, no.'

He was close to me now, his dark eyes shining with unshed tears. 'Don't leave me, Dee-Dee. Don't . . .' And then, 'I love you, Dee-Dee.'

'Oh, my *dear*.' I folded my arms around him. 'I love you too, you know that. I won't leave you, Richard.

'Promise?'

'I promise, Richard.'

And I won't, I thought. I knew I was being ill-wished, but I would fight it till it rebounded on its owner. I would not give way. For myself it didn't matter, but I would fight for Richard . . .

It was my will—and my love, against the other's.

I felt stronger, though not better. After all, I thought, every day brings us a day nearer to help coming, to us getting out. If anything was to be done to me and to Richard, it would have to be soon.

I picked up the witchcraft book again, and studied the words written on the title page,

Draw, Down the Dark Moon. Last night the moon was full, did that have any meaning? I read through the book and at last found a clue.

'*The waning, or dark moon, was the symbol of Hecate, goddess of magic. Jason was told by his mother, Aphrodite, to invoke Hecate to 'draw down the dark moon', since she herself could not work magic.*'

And underneath: *Spells are best carried out when the moon is waning.*

Was that what he was waiting for, the waning moon, to invoke power for the final effort? That must be next week. But by then we might be free.

He must be waiting for the right moment. Having to risk our being rescued . . . unless he could affect the weather too . . . there'd been a bad winter in the eighteen-eighties when Mary Dean died . . .

Seven days of a waning moon. I counted it on my calendar. The last week in January, taking us up to February . . . What had I read about February . . . ?

The witch's year began at Hallowe'en, the beginning of Nature's destruction and death. Candlemas was the end of the reign of the lord of misrule. On this day, the second of February, the fire of the old year was ceremoniously put out, new fire was kindled and blessed. The Feast of the Flame. Druids keep it with the same rite.

Seven days to keep myself alive and thus to

save Richard. Seven days to break the spell that bound Darrenscar.

I was oppressed that I seemed to be fighting something that was as old as Time itself. I was one with the ancient peoples and their festivals, held in the far off days, when they feared Nature and sought to propitiate her. As I looked at the harsh snow I understood their feeling. If I was scared, how much worse would it have been for those old ones, who knew so little, who thought it necessary to make a ritual sacrifice to appease the angry gods.

I still overslept, and I still had headaches, but I forced myself to think of Richard. He was at the forefront of my mind the whole time. I told Charles I was much better. I emphasised before them all that I was well. I tried to appear unafraid. 'We'll soon be able to get out,' I said. The village was open, via the road from Charby, we heard on the radio. A huge digger was being used to get to some of the isolated farms. Planes over the area . . .

I had a thought. Planes were flying over the area. And if someone was ill they could put out a sign, couldn't they? I could do the same, if necessary. Why hadn't Charles told me that?

I felt better.

Until the next morning. Richard said that someone had been in again, whispering Hide and Seek.

'I don't think anyone could come in,' I told

him.

'See, there's the chest behind the door.'

I went towards it. Had it been moved? Was it in the same position? I had heard nothing, but I was still sleeping heavily.

And it was the beginning of the waning, the dark moon. Only a few more days to Candlemas. Never, I thought, would any old pagan welcome the coming of the sun more gladly than I.

On Tuesday, Charles came in from feeding the chickens and one of his fruitless searches of the horizon. 'They're coming,' he said. 'I can see something in the distance . . . they're getting through . . .'

I jumped up. 'When?' I asked. 'When?'

'Tomorrow, maybe. We'll hope so.'

One more day. Or two. If anything was to happen it would have to be tonight.

I prepared dinner, Aunt Kitty taking the plates to the table. Charles fetched a bottle of wine to celebrate, but I refused to drink. I must keep a clear head. Alan spilled some salt and threw a pinch over his shoulder. 'Old superstitions die hard,' he said.

I took Richard to bed as soon as I could, and pushed the chest behind the door. No doubt it could be moved, as Alan had said, but at least I would hear.

I tried to stay awake, but I knew it was useless, my head was as heavy as lead. I put an arm firmly over Richard and held him close to me.

I was dreaming. I was walking through the snow, and Mary Dean was with me. I fell in a drift, and someone was trying to pull me out. Mary Dean vanished and I knew she had merged into myself. Someone was pulling me . . . 'No,' I said. 'Don't hurt me.'

I woke, dazed and heavy and looked round. Richard was not in the bed.

I fumbled with the matches and lit the candle. The chest had been pushed away from the door. Richard had gone.

I grabbed my dressing-gown and slippers, ran downstairs, shouting. I could see someone walking through the door, a child in its arms. It was a figure clad in an army greatcoat, a black helmet on the head. The door slammed.

'Help,' I shouted. 'Help me.' And ran downstairs.

I opened the door, grabbing the shepherd's crook as I did so. The figure was walking towards the dungeon. And Richard had nothing over his pyjamas.

I ran after the figure, and it was a nightmare on the slippery ground, a nightmare where you try to hurry but can't. The figure disappeared into the dungeon and I grabbed the door, jumped inside.

I started down the steps and a voice spoke from behind me, the figure had been waiting.

'That's right,' said the voice. 'Richard is down there, you join him. This is the way it had to be. A sacrifice. I waited for you, Mary Dean. I waited a long time. This time I've won.'

The figure turned to the door, went through, made to close it.

And I recognised the voice. I saw clearly in the snow-light the face of the murderer.

CHAPTER SEVEN

When the door closed there'd be no escape. I would die in the freezing cold. I could not see Richard, could see nothing but the closing of the dungeon and the figure looming above me, stepping outside, looking down, *smiling*.

I sprang up the steps. I wouldn't be in time, already a hand was on the door, moving it, closing it. It would have shut but for one thing. I still held the shepherd's crook, and I thrust it upwards, it caught the figure round the ankle.

There came a grunt, but I held on. I pulled myself up and we were struggling. And even as I struggled I went back. That black helmet . . . black hair, the long green dress. 'Mrs Stephen Blane,' I said. *'Aunt Kitty.'*

'Mrs Stephen Blane was a grand lady,' she said. 'As I should be. So I asked the gipsy to help, I knew she would. She wanted revenge,

171

you see; revenge on the Blane men.'

'It was you,' I gasped. 'The witchcraft, it was you.'

'I had to call the gipsy,' she said. 'I knew she was still waiting. She came, came inside me, told me what to do. Get rid of Charles, break his marriage—'

'Using your own son.' I could only whisper now. 'How could you?'

For a fractional moment her grasp slackened, her face, so close to mine, looked almost bewildered. 'But he would gain Darrenscar,' she said. 'And I'd be mistress. That's why I told Marianne to go; I knew she would die, she was so upset. The gipsy told me what to do. She helped Mrs Stephen when she practised witchcraft, but Mr Stephen was never punished for the death of Mary Dean as the gipsy intended. This time the gipsy's won, though, for I shall swear Charles took Richard and you to the dungeon. Everyone blames him for Marianne, everyone dislikes him. You yourself told Alan about your suspicions, you told Mrs Appleby.' She gave a strange weird laugh. 'Get down to Richard, he's there, down in the dungeon, in the cold, asleep.'

She was immensely strong, and she was on the outside of the door. I had to keep her out or she might murder Richard, and I had to get out, too, or we'd both die. I moaned, thinking of Richard in the cold below.

I drew in my breath and screamed. A lonely sound, it echoed over the wastes of snow, echoed and re-echoed back to the dungeon.

'You won't wake them,' she said. 'I gave them all something to make them sleep. Richard too. And you. But I woke you.'

It was incredible that she could struggle so and talk. My breath was going. It was so cold. My fingers were getting numb. She was pushing me now, back into the door. I had to put out one hand to stop myself from falling down the steps into the blackness . . . She used both hands . . . In a mighty effort to stop her my right hand came back and scratched her face, I think her forehead, I felt blood running on my hand. She grunted, and I screamed again.

And then the cock started crowing.

It went on and on without a break. I felt Aunt Kitty weakening. Had I read that to scratch a witch above the nose and mouth, and draw blood, would break her spell . . . ? Or was it that the blood was in her eyes? . . . I had to get her outside . . . So I screamed and pushed, and the cock crew. It was, I thought, hysterically, enough to wake the dead. Perhaps Charles was dead, perhaps she had poisoned him, and I'd be alone with her in this mausoleum of Darrenscar. Except for Alan . . . whose side would Alan be on?

I had dropped the shepherd's crook long ago, I didn't know where. Now I felt it in the doorway. I was panting and gasping and the cold bit into my throat, my chest. 'Please God,' I said, aloud. 'Please God, help me.'

I gave a tremendous heave, and she caught her foot in the shepherd's crook. She gave a loud cry and fell on the frozen yard, where she lay still.

'Oh, dear heaven,' I moaned. 'I've killed her.'

I crouched down beside her, whimpering. She was breathing in a loud, stertorous way. I was so exhausted by the sheer terror of the night that I wanted to lie down in the snow . . . . the world spun round me crazily . . .

And then Charles and Alan came running.

'What the hell's going on?' shouted Charles. 'What's the matter with that damned bird?'

His arms were round me, pulling me to my feet. 'Richard,' I said. 'Get Richard. He's down there. Go on . . .'

With a startled look at me he went into the dungeon. I stood, leaning on Alan.

Charles returned, Richard in his arms. The child lay still; he looked lifeless.

'Take him,' Charles said to me. 'We'll bring Aunt Kitty. Come on, Alan. Time for explanations later.'

My strength had returned with the touch of Richard's body. I hurried indoors with him. The cock had stopped now, there was an unearthly silence.

Back to the warm kitchen, grabbing a blanket to wrap Richard. Charles and Alan lay Aunt Kitty on the sofa.

'Get hot water bottles, Alan,' I said. 'Richard is so cold. And he is so still. Why doesn't he wake, Charles?'

Alan filled the bottles, gave me another blanket. I felt Richard's pulse. It was faint, but there.

'She gave him something,' I said. 'She gave us all something to make us sleep. But she woke me, led me to the dungeon. Richard was there . . .'

'Try to wake him,' Charles said, and I shook him gently. 'Richard,' I called, and louder. 'Richard. Come back to me.'

He stirred. His eyelids fluttered, then closed again. I was frantic now. 'Don't go to sleep, Richard. Richard.'

Charles went to the shelves, and returned with a glass. 'Wake him, Dee. Give him this. It will make him sick.'

Again I shook Richard. Charles crouched beside me. 'He's warmer now,' he said. 'Don't be too gentle, Dee. We've got to wake him.'

Between us we stirred Richard from his drug-induced sleep, and managed to get him to drink.

He was very sick. And his life returned. He gazed round at us, and I pressed him to me. 'Dee-Dee,' he murmured.

'He'll be all right,' Charles said. 'Take him to bed, Dee. We'll see to Aunt Kitty. I think she's had a stroke.'

I carried Richard upstairs. And it was only then that I noticed the lights were on again.

★   ★   ★

I didn't think I should sleep. I didn't think I'd ever sleep again. But when one is emotionally exhausted Nature's remedy takes over. I satisfied myself that Richard was sleeping normally, was warm, lay down beside him and knew no more till Charles knocked and entered. It was ten o'clock.

'Come, Dee,' he said, gently. 'We've been rescued. They have dug us out, literally. They've been working since first light. And I've been over to fetch the doctor. He's here now. Dr. Matthews.'

He was a youngish man who entered the room, tall and lean. I struggled up, and realised I was fully dressed. 'I didn't know I'd been to sleep,' I said, shakily. 'Please look at Richard.'

'What exactly happened?' asked the doctor.

I looked at Charles. 'Tell him, Dee,' he said. 'You know, we don't.'

'He was taken out in the night, carried outside,' I said, carefully. 'He had been given something to make him sleep, we don't know what, but he was sick, and—and—'

176

'How long was he outside?' asked the doctor.

'Oh.' I mentally reckoned up. The struggle in the dungeon had seemed hours, but it could not have been more than ten—fifteen minutes.

The doctor examined Richard thoroughly. 'I don't think there are any ill-effects,' he said. 'Keep him in bed a day or two to be sure. And now, I believe you have another patient?'

'We carried her to her room,' Charles said to me. 'If you'll take the doctor in, Dee, I'll wait downstairs.

I led the way. Aunt Kitty still lay supine. Her forehead had been bathed, but the doctor examined the scratches I had made. 'What happened?' he asked.

'I did that,' I said. 'She was taking Richard outside.'

'In the middle of the night?'

'Yes.'

'I don't suppose you know why?'

I hesitated. What to say? My head still felt muzzy. If I told the truth would Aunt Kitty be charged with attempted murder? What would Charles want me to do? I shook my head, voicelessly.

'And you went after her, struggled with her, presumably?'

'Yes. And then she fell. Have—have I hurt her?'

'Apart from the scratches, no. She has had a stroke. Let us go down.'

He left, and I made to follow, but my eye caught the writing bureau in the corner, the heap of greyish-white powder lying on a sheet of paper. I folded it carefully and picked it up. Below that was an old, yellowish piece of paper, in Mary Dean's handwriting. This I put in my pocket.

In the kitchen Alan sat, white-faced. I handed the powder to the doctor, telling him where I'd found it. He sniffed it, tasted a few specks on his finger. 'It is a herb of some kind, I would say,' he said. 'Just what, I cannot tell. Do you have any hemlock growing round here, Mr Blane?'

"*My heart aches and drowsy numbness pains my sense*"', I said.

' "*As though of hemlock I had drunk*"',' Charles finished. 'But good grief, I wouldn't know hemlock if I saw it.'

'Tall, uninteresting sort of plant,' said the doctor 'It is a sedative, and can be poisonous.'

I thought of my 'illness' of recent weeks, my over-sleeping, my headaches, sense of weakness. Somehow Aunt Kitty had sprinkled this grey powder on my food or drink.

'Was Mrs Blane in the habit of going out in the middle of the night?' asked the doctor.

'Oh, no,' Charles said, but added uncertainly. 'At least, not to my knowledge,' and I knew he was thinking of the black cockerel. That must have been killed in the night, before the heavy snow fell.

'Has she been strange lately?' persisted Dr
Matthews. 'Or was she always that way?'

'Well, she was always a sort of foolish,'
Charles said.

'And this hemlock? What was that for?'

'She was dabbling in witchcraft,' I said.

'That was very foolish of her,' said the
doctor. 'Or for any person of mental
instability.'

'Will she recover?' asked Charles.

'One never knows with this sort of thing. She
is completely paralysed now. She may regain
use, or part use, of her faculties, but I do not
hold out much hope.'

'Shouldn't she be in hospital?' Charles asked.

'Not at the moment. Our hospitals, as you
know, are very overcrowded. Unless you can
afford a private nursing home.'

'Given the news I've had this morning, that
all my sheep are dead,' Charles said, harshly,
'that's just what I can't do.'

'H'm. Then perhaps a nurse? Mrs Blane does
not require a great deal of nursing, she can be
fed, liquids, of course. But in view of what you
have told me I think it would be better to have a
trained nurse looking after her.'

'Yes,' Charles agreed. 'Do you know of
anyone?'

'There is a Mrs Chant, in Middlesborough,'
Dr Matthews said. 'A widow, went back to

nursing when her husband died. She is free now, I think. Shall I try to get her for you?'

'Please.'

'I'll get in touch immediately, and ring you.'

'Yes, our phone is working now. Thank you, Doctor.'

We sat in the kitchen as the doctor's car drove away. 'I couldn't tell him everything, could I?' I asked.

Charles faced me. 'What can I say, Dee? Aunt Kitty always seemed such a harmless old soul, if dotty—'

'That was what she intended,' I replied. 'She planned it all, right from the beginning. She was always pottering around the yard, feeding her chickens. But when she took Richard to the dungeon the first time, she knew I'd get him out. That was what she wanted, for me to suspect you.'

'She meant to put the blame on me . . . Why?'

'To claim Darrenscar for Alan. She practised witchcraft, invoked the gipsy, or so she said.' I repeated what Aunt Kitty had told me. 'The gipsy wanted to destroy the master of the house, not by death, but by punishment for death. It seems Mrs Stephen Blane practised witchcraft, too. Aunt Kitty learned of this, found her book on the Black Art, did as she did, wanting to be like her, becoming her at times.' I drew a shuddering breath. 'So—if you were sent to jail, Charles, Alan would have Darrenscar. To that end Aunt Kitty told Marianne to go, after the quarrel. Aunt Kitty, not you.'

'I didn't know,' Alan whispered. 'You believe me?'

'Of course,' Charles answered. 'She fooled us all.'

'Just how much did she fool you?' I asked. 'Who told you that Marianne was having an affair with Alan, Charles?'

'Why—good heavens, she did. But it was all done so accidentally.'

'Naturally.'

'I remember well. She brought me tea in the study. I said I'd take it in the kitchen to Marianne, for I was hoping, even then, that we could make up. She appeared flustered, said Marianne was upstairs in her bedroom. I said I'd go up to her. Aunt Kitty said no, better not. And then it all came out. Marianne was with Alan. She wouldn't have told me for the world, but—'

'And you went up and caught them,' I said.

'Yes.'

'And you were furious and attacked Alan. Badly. And you thought afterwards you were possessed. Did she tell you that?'

'I don't remember. I—I was so ashamed that I'd lost my temper in that way.'

'We can guess,' I said. 'She brought you up,

181

after all.'

'But Stephen Blane must have killed Mary Dean,' he said.

'Oh no, Charles. Here is the paper I found in Aunt Kitty's room. The last pages of Mary Dean's diary.'

I spread out the paper.

The writing was large, straggly, as if indeed it had been written in the dark, in anguish and in pain. Some of the words almost went off the page. But it was readable.

'Now I understand all. Mrs Blane persuaded Stephen to keep me here—he did not know that she practised witchcraft. I know now that she wants my unbaptised baby for her unholy rites. It is too late for me to go to the village now the pains are upon me: there is only one way to save my baby from her. I have come down here, alone, to this awful place that is never used. We shall be buried alive, he and I, and when we are found—if ever—it will be too late for her to use him. I shall baptise the child myself with the sign of the cross, and may God have mercy on our souls . . .

Mary Dean.'

'But the coachman found them,' I said.

'And I suppose,' Charles ruminated, 'Stephen Blane suppressed the paper to protect his wife.'

'And to protect Mary Dean,' I said. 'As a suicide she would not have been buried in consecrated ground, and he knew how much she would want that. That's why he said he'd baptised the baby.'

'Poor Mary Dean,' said Charles.

'Yes, because she wasn't a suicide so much as one who sacrificed her life for her child. I don't think she did really love Robert; she wanted his position, but she did not want the child. Not till it was too late did she begin to think about it, that's why she said: "*If only I could have another chance to love you as I should.*" It was her dying wish.'

Charles sighed, and I went on. 'What happened to Mrs Blane, Charles. Do you know?'

'No. It was all rather mysterious. Robert died abroad, left no children, so his wife presumably went back to her parents. Some time after Mary Dean died, Stephen also died, of a fever, and his wife seemed to have disappeared, there is no mention of what happened to her, that's why I could not bring the history up to date. The children were away at school, and had a guardian, a solicitor, as there didn't seem to be any relatives around. That's all we know.'

I went up to Richard, pondering. And as I passed Aunt Kitty's door I knew that the pattern was not broken yet.

* * *

Mrs Chant came that evening, an older woman,

quiet, not given to talking. I put her in my old room, and she asked if she could see her patient.

I led her to Aunt Kitty's room, and we both gazed at the figure on the bed. She lay, paralysed, her arms by her side, but whereas earlier her eyes had been closed, now they were open, and seemed to glare at me balefully. I shivered.

Outside again, I said to Mrs Chant: 'The doctor told you all about her, I imagine? That she dabbled in witchcraft?'

'That was very foolish,' said Mrs Chant, unperturbed.

'She—she tried to kill me. You're not afraid?'

'No. I am used to nursing mental patients.'

'You don't believe me, do you, about the witchcraft?' I asked.

She did not answer directly. 'What kind of woman was she?' she asked. 'What kind of girl?'

'I haven't known her long, so I can only repeat what I've been told. She said they called her Kitten when she was a girl. I can understand that, some of it lingers yet. But then the other takes over, and she pretends to be a former Mrs Blane, a grand lady . . .' I shivered suddenly. *Was it pretence?* Was she a reincarnation of Mrs Stephen, calling on the gipsy as before . . .'

'Supposing she should recover?' I asked.

'I think that's very unlikely. But don't worry, I have strict instructions from Dr Matthews to ring him the moment any sign of recovery takes place.'

We walked along towards the bathroom, and she patted my arm. 'Don't worry, Miss Martin, she can't do any more harm.'

'Call me Dee,' I said, and left her.

But as I went downstairs I knew with foreboding that I should never know any peace while Aunt Kitty remained in the house. For if she *did* recover . . . ?

The bombshell fell that evening. Dinner was over, Mrs Chant had gone to Aunt Kitty, Richard was asleep, we sat, Charles, Alan and I.

Alan had hardly spoken all day. Now he said: 'Charles, I'm going away.'

Charles looked up. I stared. 'Going away? You mean for a holiday?' Charles asked.

'No, I mean for good. I'm sorry, Charles, to leave my mother in your care, you can take my inheritance for that.'

'But why?' I asked.

'I can't explain. Something's gone out of me. All this means nothing to me now.'

'It's shock,' Charles said, gruffly. 'Wait a little while—'

'It's true I did have a shock,' Alan said. 'When I learned about my mother . . . I've been thinking about it all day. I've even been wondering if I'm right in thinking that she threw Marianne and me together . . .'

'From what we now know it seems pretty certain,' Charles said. 'Though I suppose the baby upset even her calculations.'

Alan said in a low voice, 'I know you'll never believe me, Charles, but the child is not mine. It's true that on one or two occasions Marianne and I—did make love—and I'm sorry, but not—not at that time. My mother wanted me to claim him as my own, otherwise he'd be your heir . . .'

'It's no use going over all that,' Charles said, wearily. 'I lost my temper and I'm sorry, but I'm willing to bring the boy up as my own. There's no need for you to go.'

'I want to go.'

'And lose your inheritance?'

'Hasn't there been enough trouble caused by these stupid inheritances? It's been the cause of much of the Blanes' trouble, certainly of my mother's . . . trouble. She wanted money and was prepared to go to any lengths . . . I want no part in it.'

'But where will you go?' Charles asked.

'To Australia.'

'Australia? Just like that.'

'I know a fellow there, met him at college, we've always kept in touch. He's doing well, he'll vouch for me, sponsor me, give me a job.'

'What does he do?' Charles asked.

'He has a sheep farm. Oh, I know what

you're going to say, I couldn't even look after our own sheep . . . Charles, I'm sorry about that.'

'At least,' Charles said, reflectively, 'you wouldn't have your mother egging you on to mischief. Oh, I knew she did that, and it just made it harder for me, to fight the two of you.'

'I hadn't realised just what a weak pawn I was,' Alan said with some bitterness. 'Now you see why I must go.'

Charles sighed. 'If you must.'

'The pattern really is breaking,' I thought.

'You needn't worry about the money,' Charles said. 'I'll see you get it.'

Alan replied, 'I don't want it, Charles. I want nothing from Darrenscar.'

There was a pause, then he said, and there was almost a sob in his voice. 'Don't you understand how I feel? This . . . black witch was my mother . . .'

His face looked young and boyish. 'No, Alan,' I said, gently. 'Your mother was the young girl they called Kitten because she was playful and loving.'

But I loved him for breaking free.

*　　　*　　　*

There was a thaw on Candlemas Day all over the country. Houses were flooded, pipes burst, rivers overflowed. Our road was clear, but snow

187

still lay on the High Moor. Alan came to see me before he left.

'I'm sorry, Dee,' he said.

'You mean this is goodbye?'

'I did love you,' he said. 'But now it all seems part of a dream. Yes, that's how it seems, a dream.'

I watched him walk away to the car, which he intended to sell in London before he left. He waved once, and was gone.

I turned and closed the door. It was still very cold. And Charles, behind me, said: 'Don't cry for him, Dee.'

'I won't', I said. 'But he was nice, underneath, Charles.'

*   *   *

So we entered a strange period at Darrenscar. In some ways a dull period, except that, for me, the fear was always underneath, even yet. Mrs Chant did not take a regular day off as, she said, she had no family to visit, she merely let us know when she wanted a few hours off for shopping, or a walk. Then it would be my duty to look in on Aunt Kitty, a job I feared. I would enter the room, see those eyes follow me balefully, and wonder if she would recover.

Mrs Chant told me not to worry. But as I watched Aunt Kitty's eyes I still felt a certain power emanating from her, and I was afraid.

How much, after all, did Mrs Chant understand about the dark moon? She seemed to be able to sense Aunt Kitty's requirements, and I asked her one day if she thought Aunt Kitty could hear. 'I'm sure of it,' was the reply.

'But she can't speak?'

'No, but she has a way of looking at me in a certain manner, and I know what it is she needs.'

I was disquieted. I had an odd feeling that Aunt Kitty was waiting—for what?

'I suppose she knows Alan's gone?' I said.

'Oh, yes. And she misses him.'

I missed him, too. Darrenscar seemed empty without him. I told myself he was no good, but it did not affect my heart. And when a letter arrived for me from Australia I could hardly wait to open it.

'*Dear Dee*,' I read,

'I like it here, and I'm settling down well. Tell Charles I am working hard. I was determined, you see, when I came out to do just that. I like the life, I like the country. I feel altogether different. It's like being reborn.'

I pondered that last sentence for a long time.

The winter dragged on, cold and icy, yet there was beauty in the white moors, majestic, aloof. How many hundreds of years had they watched men come and go? I thought of the old saw 'York was founded when King David ruled Jerusalem.' Had the Romans walked on these moors, even before the Vikings came? The very weight of its age pressed on me.

Spring came, still cold and wet, and washed away much of the snow. I was able to get out again and the first thing I did was to go to the village, brave with blowing daffodils and colourful crocus, and call on Mrs Appleby. She was glad to see me, and I told her about Mrs Blane, the stroke, and Alan. She clucked about the loss of the sheep.

'Charles should sell that land,' she said, as she handed me tea in a pretty china cup.

'You know about it?' I asked, astonished.

'The village has been talking about nothing else for months. There's been talk, and meetings. Angry meetings. You see, we need houses here, built for us, not for faraway people who come only once a year and then shut them up. Houses our young people can afford.'

'But could they get to work?'

'They can manage that with a new road. Please God we won't have another winter like last one for some time.'

'But Charles wouldn't be building the houses.'

'He could make that a stipulation of the sale. Don't you worry, if Charles insisted that's what he wanted, then it would be done.'

'And you think he won't?' I ate my cake, pondering. 'Tell me,' I said. 'Why is there so much bitterness against the Blanes?'

'They were never good employers, and then there were all the funny goings-on. They'd never do anything to help the villagers and folks think Charles is the same. Why should he care what houses are built, so long as he has the money?'

When I went back to Darrenscar I was thoughtful.

Richard continued to improve, and the doctor was pleased. Charles still worked in the study all day, he had started a new book; but he no longer shut himself away at night, we would sit together in the kitchen, usually alone.

He began to talk to me, diffidently at first, and I understood for the first time that his taciturnity was simply a lack of the ability to communicate with anyone, caused no doubt by the fact that he'd never had anyone to confide in; in all his life he'd had to shoulder burdens alone . . . But what about Marianne? Had her beauty stunned him into silence, made her a goddess, unapproachable? I was no goddess, I thought ruefully, just a common or garden typist cum home help. But I confided in him, I told him about Aunt Meg, my feeling of not belonging, the sense of loss I seemed to carry all my early life. We found we had a lot in common, we both liked poetry, drives and walks in the country, history, we disliked parties, 'trendiness' . . .

And gradually we talked about Darrenscar,

the pattern. 'I really felt,' he said, painfully, 'that I was possessed. I suppose I always hid my feelings, and then when I learned about Alan I—I felt I wanted to kill him. That frightened me. So that when you talked about taking Richard to the dungeon I did wonder if I had done it without knowing . . . Then the black cockerel, I didn't want to say too much about that, knowing you were scared, but it had been killed the night before, the blood was dry . . . and I knew what it meant. But how did I know I hadn't gone out in the night?'

'Poor Charles,' I said. 'If we had died in the dungeon, it would have been so easy for her to put the blame on you.'

'Very easy. For I would have half believed it myself.'

'One thing I don't understand,' I said. 'That book on witchcraft with Stephen Blane's signature inside, and later the words Draw Down the Dark Moon in the same writing . . . ?'

'Signatures can be imitated,' said Charles. 'First to throw Mary Dean off the scent, and later to frighten you. But that's not important now. What is important—' he hesitated.

'Yes?' I asked.

'. . . is what's always been important—trying to keep this place going. Now I've lost the sheep—'

'Why don't you sell the land?' I asked.

'You think I should?'

'The village does,' I told him. 'If you built for them, that is.'

'If I sold the land I'd have no say in what was built.'

'You could make that stipulation.'

'I think,' he said, 'I'd prefer holiday bungalows. At least I'd not see much of people that way.'

I stared at him. So he was still afraid to meet people. I chose my words carefully. 'Try to think about the villagers,' I said. 'They do need houses very badly, and they are your neighbours, after all.'

'I don't really see why I should.'

'Because of the bitterness that still goes on after all these years. And you could break it. You don't have to, I know, you have no responsibility at all towards the village. It's just a matter of being friends.'

He moved restlessly. 'You know I don't want to meet people.'

'Nice if you can afford it, Charles.' I turned to face him. 'I think it's time you started forgetting Marianne. You're shutting yourself away like a Victorian miss going into a decline. But all you'll become is a grumpy old recluse.'

He laughed then. 'I like you, Dee,' he said. 'You really bring me down to earth. But it isn't just Marianne, it's—' he stopped. 'It's resentment,' he finished.

'Against whom?'

'Alan, of course. And the odd thing is I've only just realised it. I always resented him, his ability to sail through life with the minimum of effort, while there was I, the old work-horse . . . And then Marianne . . . Even you loved him, Dee.'

'Yes,' I said.

'We'll have to console each other.'

'I don't—' I stopped. I was about to say, 'I don't want to be consoled, I don't want to be second-best to Marianne.' But I thought over Alan's words. 'It's like being reborn.' Perhaps we'd all have to do that. Perhaps everyone did when they started a new page in their lives.

Aloud I said, 'The pattern's breaking, isn't it?'

'Shouldn't you say, broken?'

'No, not yet, Charles. We still don't know what the gipsy meant when she said there was only one thing that would break the pattern. Charles—I'm still afraid of Aunt Kitty.'

'She can't hurt you now, Dee.'

'It's uncanny,' I said. 'The way she is able to make Mrs Chant understand what she wants, how she makes her do things . . . sometimes I wonder if she is as paralysed as she pretends.'

'The doctor sees her. He's satisfied.'

'Yes.' I moved, restlessly. 'But if she recovers—'

'You really are scared, aren't you? Naturally,

I suppose. After the dungeon episode . . . you think she might try to kill you again?'

'And Richard,' I said.

He was silent for quite a time. Then he said: 'I must get her into a private nursing home. I could do that, if the land was sold.' He came towards me, put his hands on my shoulders. 'Would that make you happier, Dee?'

'Oh yes,' I said.

'Then I'll do it,' he nodded. 'Not for the village, but for you.'

I was suddenly happy that someone should do such a thing for me. I asked, 'But you'll build the houses the village want?'

'I will,' he said. 'And will no doubt be the first Blane to be a local benefactor.'

'They'll bless you for it,' I said. 'For the first time since the seventeenth century, you'll be accepted.'

'You're a terrible bully,' he grumbled.

'I know,' I said. 'I'm developing a taste for it. But, Charles—'

He looked at me.

'Thanks,' I said.

We said no more, but we had entered a new relationship, Charles and I. We started going out together, in the afternoons, when we could take Richard. Neither of us cared too much about dining and dancing, a drive in the country was enough, and I was still nervous of leaving Richard.

195

Maybe I was foolish. But although I kept away from Aunt Kitty's room, I was forced to go in when Mrs Chant had time off. She lay as usual, unmoving, but her eyes followed me always.

*   *   *

Alas for our hopes. The property developers who had been so keen to buy the land refused point-blank to change their plans for luxury bungalows. Charles told me one summer evening, as the moors lay bathed in the westering sun.

'So what will you do?' I asked.

He looked worried. 'Find another builder,—I hope.'

I hoped so, too. Charles advertised the land, but no one rushed to buy. It was too remote, said one, not worth the expense, said another.

Charles said little at this time, but his brow grew more furrowed, and I wondered if I was doing right to plead for small houses for the villagers. I had wanted so much to heal the breach between the village and Darrenscar, but if a builder could not be found then things would be worse then ever; there'd be no sale, no houses, and no money to pay for Aunt Kitty's nursing home.

Maybe, I thought, I should try to overcome my fears and suggest that she stay at

Darrenscar. But I noticed that Mrs Chant seemed to be showing signs of strain; she looked tired, and if we had another winter like the last, would she be willing to stay on? And my fear was still there, the fear that Aunt Kitty was not as ill as she pretended.

I was sleeping badly, and I suppose this showed, for Charles asked me one morning what was the matter. I stammered out my worries. Was I wrong to insist on the houses for the village, to send Aunt Kitty away?

He put his hands on my shoulders. 'You're not wrong,' he said. 'I told you I would get this done, and I shall, sooner or later. I have even found a nursing home willing to take Aunt Kitty as soon as the land is sold.'

And I was again filled with the feeling of gratitude, so much so that I stod quite still, lips parted.

He asked. 'What is it, Dee?'

I looked at him. 'I said once that Alan was kind. I thought he was, and you were not. Now I see that I was wrong. You are kind.'

'Dee, you're not crying?'

'Not really. It's just that kindness is fairly new to me, you see.'

'My poor Dee.' And his arms went round me, and he kissed me gently.

I realised that I could love this man. A new love, a new pattern. Not the full-blown love that burst into flower the moment I saw Alan, but something tentative, trembling on the edge of discovery. And I saw it was the same for him, too.

★   ★   ★

It was in the autumn when I ran down to the village to get a few small groceries from the shop. I had lingered, telling them Charles' problems with finding a builder, and it was nearly six when I returned, quite dark. I realised it was Hallowe'en.

I parked the car and walked towards the house. I could see Charles and Richard in the kitchen. Upstairs, the two bedrooms were lit. Mrs Chant, who had moved into Alan's room when he left, sat at a writing desk in the window, her curtains drawn back, I could see her clearly. My gaze turned to the other room, Aunt Kitty's, which had an old-fashioned blind. And clearly silhouetted on this blind, with the glow of a table-lamp at her side, was the figure of a woman, standing.

I looked back at Mrs Chant, then I was racing in the house, and upstairs, knocking at her door, bursting in. 'It's me, Mrs Chant. Aunt Kitty—is she better?'

Mrs Chant stood up, startled. 'Better? I left her asleep half an hour ago.'

We ran into the next room, opened the door. Aunt Kitty lay still as always. She was not asleep and her eyes looked mockingly into mine.

'I tell you I saw her,' I said, but Mrs Chant replied, 'Impossible. It must have been a reflection of something else.'

I went down again, outside, and looked up at the window. There was no shadow now.

I dreaded the winter. I was afraid it might be like last year's, that we'd be cut off, alone . . . I firmly believed that Aunt Kitty had been standing that night, but Mrs Chant said it was not possible, and the doctor agreed when he came. I wondered again if Aunt Kitty had the power to pretend to be paralysed, that she was waiting . . . I even fancied I saw a veiled triumph in her eyes when I went in to look at her, but I said nothing of this to Charles.

It was just before Christmas when the good news came. My talk to the villagers on Hallowe'en had had results, they had taken matters into their own hands and found a builder, an ex-local man. Not a large developer, but one with enough capital to buy, and willing to build what we wanted. Charles told me about it and I let out my breath in a deep sigh.

'Two more months and it will all be settled,' he said. 'The nursing home will take Aunt Kitty at the end of February. So now let's go out and celebrate.'

We took Richard into York. The weather was quite mild for December, and we went round the shops, bought presents. Richard, who was, as the doctor had promised, practically normal now for his age, skipped along between us. Charles asked him if he would like to visit the Railway Museum.

'Oooh, yes.' Richard certainly had the normal boy's love of trains, I thought. So had Charles.

I trailed along behind, Charles explaining to Richard the history of the railways, seeing the old locomotives, the railway equipment, working models. And as we left, Charles picked Richard up in his arms and we crossed to a small restaurant, where he was placed in a chair.

'Well, Richard,' Charles said. 'Did you enjoy that?'

'Yes, Dad.' The word was entirely natural, and unselfconscious. I saw Charles look at him, open his mouth to say something, change his mind, and let a small pleased smile cover his face. Another acceptance for Charles, I thought.

We ate our meal, chatting about the day. And when it was over Charles said to me: 'I haven't bought you a present yet, Dee. What would you like?'

'Oh—I don't know,' I murmured.

He looked at Richard's happy face. 'You know,' he said. 'I've been thinking. I've enjoyed today so much. Have you?'

'Yes, Charles.'

'I'd never have done this sort of thing with

Marianne. Oh, don't get me wrong, it wasn't her fault so much as mine. I—' he moved his coffee-cup in its saucer as if it were most important to get it quite straight. 'I think I fell in love with Marianne's beauty. And—on the one hand I neglected her while I worked, yet I wanted to shut her up for my own eyes alone. The original male chauvinist pig, wouldn't you say? No wonder she turned to Alan. I didn't realise that a man needs more than that from the woman he intends to go through life with; he needs someone to talk to—you taught me that.'

'Makes me sound rather dull,' I commented.

'It shouldn't. I'd want to make love to you as well.'

The atmosphere between us was suddenly charged. I looked at him, but was unable to hold my gaze. His hand closed over mine.

'Have you forgotten Alan?' he asked.

'No,' I said. 'And I never will. We were old lovers, Charles, from long ago. Perhaps when King David ruled Jerusalem. But it's over now.'

'Supposing he should come back?'

'He won't,' I said, flatly. 'Perhaps he's the one that always gets away—the dream that never comes true.'

'And you'll spend your life dreaming about him.'

'No. The dream was before I met him. Now I

can start again.'

'Can you, Dee? Can you let Mary Dean go now?'

'I'll try,' I said.

'Could you love me?'

'Yes, Charles.'

'Could you marry me?'

'Yes, Charles.'

He leaned towards me and there, in the crowded restaurant, he kissed me. And for a short space of time the world disappeared, and Alan was forgotten.

Then Richard banged the table with a spoon, and we both turned to him laughing. 'Kiss me,' he shouted.

'Richard,' Charles said. 'How would you like Dee to be your new mother, never to leave you again?'

'Oh, yes,' Richard said, and banged harder than ever. And people stared and laughed, and we laughed, and then went out to buy an engagement ring.

In the car, before we started for home, Charles put both his arms around me and kissed me deeply. I responded. And I realised that he was a passionate man, as Alan was not, and that I could give him more than Marianne could, for all her beauty.

We went home laden with gifts, and me with a sapphire and diamond ring on my finger. We burst into the kitchen and Charles opened a bottle of champagne. He called Mrs Chant, and we gave her a smart handbag.

'Now we're going to celebrate,' he said, filling our glasses. 'Dee and I are engaged.'

'Why, that's wonderful,' Mrs Chant said. 'I do hope you'll be very happy.'

Charles raised his glass. 'To the future mistress of Darrenscar.'

And I watched him. I knew, with a dread feeling of certainty, that I would never be mistress of Darrenscar.

Mrs Chant went back to Aunt Kitty, and Charles came to me. 'What is it, Dee?'

'Nothing.'

'You're still afraid?'

'I suppose so.'

'It won't be long now. Aunt Kitty goes at the end of February. When shall we have the wedding? Soon?'

'I think I'd rather wait till she's gone.'

'Wouldn't you feel safer if I were protecting you?'

'Yes, I suppose so.'

'Then why wait? You don't want a big show, do you?'

'No. Well, in a few weeks, then.'

'The end of January?'

'No,' I said. 'The beginning of February. Candlemas Day.'

'Why on earth Candlemas Day?'

'The ceremony of the flame,' I said. 'The end

of the old year, the lighting of the new fire.'

'Dee, let it go now.'

'That's what I am doing. That's when it will go, all the past.'

'Very well, February the what? 2nd? A registry office in York, m'm? No fuss, no frills.

'I must tell Aunt Meg,' I said. 'You will have to meet her, Charles, she is my only relative.' I laughed. 'Aunt Kitty would be most dismayed at your marrying your home help.'

'My dear, I'm merely providing myself with a home help for life.'

'Don't bank on it,' I said. 'I might develop ideas above my station—' The rest was smothered in a kiss.

Christmas preparations went ahead, and I would have been perfectly content if it had not been that I could feel Aunt Kitty's presence, even though she was upstairs, far from the kitchen. I thought Mrs Chant had changed, she looked tired, and spent most of her time with Aunt Kitty. Sometimes I would go past the room and hear her talking, and I mentioned this to her. 'I just tell her all the news,' she said.

'Did you—tell her about our engagement?' I asked.

'Yes, of course. Why shouldn't I?'

'It doesn't matter.' But I wished she hadn't.

We were happy at Christmas. After the flurry of present-giving in the morning, and the dinner, we took Richard to the children's service in the church at Charby. I wondered if I should ask the Vicar to call and see Aunt Kitty, if he could help. But we only exchanged a few words, and somehow the moment passed. Later I wished I had.

Before Christmas was over we called to see Mrs Appleby to tell her the news. The sight of Charles entering the small house must have been seen by everyone, for suddenly the little parlour was filled with neighbours who had just 'dropped in', who talked about the new houses, and shook Charles' hand, congratulating him.

'We're no longer foreigners,' I said as we left. 'Even if I do come from London.'

'You haven't had long to wait,' Charles said, ruefully. 'For me, it's been three hundred years.'

Then back to Darrenscar, and Charles working again, while I waited. Now, when I looked in on Aunt Kitty while Mrs Chant went for a walk, as I met those bold, searching eyes, I could not hide the fear in mine, and I saw the expression in hers change to triumph. A few days later Mrs Chant announced that she needed something from the village shop, and the same thing happened between Aunt Kitty and me, and I knew that she enjoyed my fear, she fed on it. Mrs Chant came back and I asked her if she'd got what she wanted. A vague look came into her eyes. 'I don't remember what I went for,' she said, uncertainly.

I thought of my wedding, so soon to take place. We would go to York, Charles, Richard and I, we'd stay for the day, have a meal, and return.

I began to count the days. January, and the moors blown by gales, some snow and frost, though nothing so bad as last year. Days when Richard played happily, when Charles came from his study to sit close and talk. Days when Mrs Chant went to the village and I was left with Aunt Kitty and her triumphant eyes looking at my fear. Cold days, but invigorating frosts at night and a still moon.

Drawn down the dark moon. This time last year . . . I shuddered.

The last week in January. I knew there was something I had to do, one final task, but I did not know what it was. I wandered round as vaguely as Mrs Chant, who was going out now nearly every day, and seemed at a loss to understand why. Snow outside, and I was drawn against my will to Aunt Kitty's room, to drop my eyes in fear as she watched me. Then I would go back to my room where I could stand watching the trees, wondering if they were waving . . .

Friday, the day before my wedding. A cold day, with a wind blowing sleet over the bleak moors. I went into the study, to Charles, and he held me silently, feeling my unease, not knowing the cause.

'It will be all right, Dee, ' he said, softly. 'Everything will be all right.' He kissed me, and I felt an upsurge of love for him. 'I know,' I said. 'I know, Charles.'

Buoyed by our love I went upstairs. Mrs Chant had gone to the village, and I entered Aunt Kitty's room so silently that she did not hear. She lay, supine, her eyes closed, and I tiptoed nearer, looking down at the still face that, without the bold eyes, held even yet a trace of the long-ago girlishness. What had happened to the young Kitten-girl? I wondered. Why, I asked her silently, did you allow evil to take over? There must have been a moment when you could choose.

Suddenly, I was overwhelmed by pity. She had loved evil and what had it done to her? She had lost her son, as she was bound to do, because she had wanted to possess him utterly, bend his will to hers, just as she had with Richard, before the evil domination completely took over.

She opened her eyes, and I looked down at her, still pitying, and smoothed back the bedclothes. She seemed to shrink beneath them.

I went down, back to the study again, to Charles. He stood up. 'That's better,' he said. 'You look quite radiant.'

'Do I, Charles?'

He took my hands. 'That thing the gipsy

talked about, the one thing that could break the pattern . . . I know what it is. Love.'

I didn't speak.

'That's what you brought us, Dee,' he said. 'Think about it.'

'I didn't bring it here,' I said, soberly. 'I learned it.'

The next morning we were up early, and drove to York with Richard. We were married, and then to a hotel for lunch. The hotel overlooked the river, and we sat for a long time, talking desultorily, holding hands. It was a clear, cold day and the water was grey, shot with light. Richard begged for another visit to the Railway Museum, and we took him, smiling at his enjoyment. Then an early dinner, and we went to the car.

'I'm not sure if a visit to a railway museum is the done thing for a wedding day,' Charles said, ruefully.

'It's been a heavenly day,' I said.

'And now our honeymoon starts,' Charles replied. 'Did I ever tell you how lovely you were, Dee?' And his arms were round me, his kisses were deep.

We sat close on the way back, my hand rested on his arm. Richard was asleep, well wrapped in rugs. We drove silently for the most part, out of York, through the still country, up towards the moors. There was no moon.

We turned off the main road towards

Darrenscar. And then we saw it, a red glow in the sky, shooting flames . . .

'What's that?' Charles asked. 'The village? Haystacks?'

We both knew that it wasn't the village, and that there were no haystacks on the moors. We knew it was Darrenscar.

We came to the top of the hill and now we saw it clearly. Little figures running, fire engines. And a great red blaze.

Charles braked sharply, jumped out, and ran towards the house. After a quick look at Richard, I followed. There were a number of village people, a policeman . . .

Then Mrs Chant came running towards us. 'Oh, Mr Blane,' she gasped. 'I went out for a walk, I felt I had to, I had a headache . . . I was nearly at the village when I saw the fire . . . Mrs Blane was asleep when I left, and—it was too late, we couldn't get in.'

'You mean—she's still in there?' Charles asked.

'How could it have started?' Mrs Chant wailed, distraught. 'I've never left her before on her own, but I felt I had to go—' the flickering fire lit up her bewildered face. 'I'll never forgive myself.'

I leaned forward. 'I understand,' I said. 'I felt we had to go today, too.'

The flames leaped and crackled, Darrenscar was but a shell now. One of the fire officers, face blackened, came to us. 'Nothing we could do,' he said. 'It went up like tinder. Bit of a puzzle really, I wouldn't have expected it in this weather, and a well-built place like that. When we arrived it was half gone.'

'And my aunt?' Charles asked through dry lips.

'Some of the men tried to get in. It was hopeless from the start. If there was anyone inside she'd never have lived through that.'

The heat of the fire reached us even where we stood. A beam fell with a thud, and then another. The blaze went on and on, the water pouring from the firemen's hoses might have been petrol adding to the inferno. And then, suddenly, there was nothing.

I had been right, I would never be mistress of Darrenscar.

We spent our wedding night at an inn in Charby, the same one where Alan and I had lunched a year ago. An inquest was held, and we heard that the remains of Aunt Kitty's body had been found in the kitchen, fully dressed, for some remnants of clothing still adhered to her. She had been pinned to the wall by one of the beams which fell through her body, through her heart.

The fire had started in the kitchen, and the fire officer said that the house burnt as though it had been soaked in paraffin, though no traces of any such liquids had been discovered. Mrs

Chant was absolved from blame, the doctor talked about hysterical paralysis, and said that this was an interesting case. Since Mrs Blane's death, he had learned that she had dabbled in witchcraft, and this, to a person of her mental instability, would be enough to derange her completely. But as no one had seen her since her remarkable recovery, if this had indeed taken place, they could only guess at her recent state of mind. Thoughts of a break-in were pondered, but who would want to dress a paralysed woman and take her to the kitchen before setting fire to the house? There were no answers, and a puzzled jury returned a verdict of accidental death.

I wondered what would have happened if I had jumped up and said: 'Aunt Kitty had not been paralysed for a long time, but she could imitate paralysis for her own ends. She willed Mrs Chant to go out, as she had been willing her for some time to do as she wished. But her powers were waning. Whether she planned to leave the house I am not sure. I remember she said once she would sell her soul to get away. But she had already sold her soul, and the powers she served would not let her go—the beam caught her and she died. Maybe the fire was a parting gift for Charles—Alan would never have Darrenscar now, so she didn't intend that Charles should. Or maybe she had, right at the end, tried to make amends. Charles

211

had received a sealed letter from the solicitors, marked *"To be Opened upon the Destruction of Darrenscar"*. Written by Geoffrey Blane, it said that in the event of such destruction by fire, the entail would be broken, whether Darrenscar was rebuilt or not. Maybe she knew that, too, and wanted to set us free.'

I said nothing.

When it was all over, Charles and I sat talking in the little inn, next to the window with the view over the moors. He said, 'Do you know, Dee, apart from the horrible way Aunt Kitty died, and the trouble for poor Mrs Chant, I'd almost be glad.'

'Glad?'

'To lose Darrenscar. Alan was right, you know, there was so much trouble . . . it was never a happy house. I remember once going on holiday, visiting one of those monasteries where they make wine or something, and how I was struck by the absolute peace of the place. I understand now, all the prayers that were said left the legacy of peace. At Darrenscar the opposite happened. All the anger, the evil, the lust for money lingered on. It's better gone.'

I agreed. Mary Dean was buried with the ashes of Darrenscar, the pattern finally broken.

'What will we do now,' Charles?' I asked.

He sighed. 'My new book was in there, I'll have to start it again. My publisher knows someone who could rent me a cottage for the time being. Maybe later I'll rebuild a new house for us, a pleasant house to hold happy memories . . .'

*   *   *

We are living in the cottage now, in the south of England, temporarily, while Charles rewrites his book. Then we shall go back, for pleasant as this soft countryside is, we both miss the stark beauty of the moors. We are planning our future home, not big, nothing pretentious, not even too isolated, perhaps near those already being built for the villagers. Ours, we hope, will be a house of happiness, with children running in the gardens, playing with Richard, riding a small sturdy pony. Shining windows outside, and inside, love.

But to be on the safe side I shall plant a rowan tree at the gate.

Photoset, printed and bound in Great Britain by REDWOOD BURN LIMITED, Trowbridge, Wiltshire